THE Fountain OF Highlandtown

THE *Fountain* OF *Highlandtown*

STORIES BY
RAFAEL ALVAREZ

WOODHOLME
HOUSE
PUBLISHERS

Baltimore, Maryland

Printed and bound in the United States of America.

1 2 3 4 5   06 05 04 03 02 01 00 99 98 97

Library of Congress Cataloging-in-Publication Data

Alvarez, Rafael, 1958–
  The fountain of Highlandtown : stories / by Rafael Alvarez.
  p.   cm.
  ISBN 0-9656342-8-0
  1. City and town life—Maryland—Baltimore—Fiction. 2. Baltimore (Md.)
  —Social life and customs—Fiction. I. Title.
  PS3551.L848F68 1997
  813'.54—dc21   97-20253
                                                           CIP

Woodholme House Publishers
1829 Reisterstown Road
Suite 130
Baltimore, Maryland 21208
Fax: (410) 653-7904
Orders: 1-800-488-0051

Book design: Brushwood Graphics, Inc.
Cover design: Nancy Johnston
Cover art: Jonathon Scott Fuqua
Backcover photograph: Jim Burger

In honor of
Gloria and Manuel
my mother and father

Contents

Introduction

In my time wandering the streets of Baltimore, I have consulted gin-mill gurus and paint-brush swamis, trudging
through brown fields of dust and feathers to have what no
one would keep me from having.

—*From "The Flap Doodle"*

WHAT CAN YOU SAY about a collection of short stories in which
a love-crazed Baltimore junkman—Orlo Pound—serves up jumbo-
sized helpings of "pig's feet simmered soft in a thin broth of tomato
and basil" to the great love of his life, the tormented Leini, while the
fragrant aroma of "slow-cooked pork" mixes with "the stench of
molten steel" before blowing back to the city on crosswinds of the
Patapsco?

How can you characterize a work of fiction in which a girl named
Lulu stands hypnotized, transfixed by an immense "whirli-gig" looming high above Key Highway, "a giant egg beater glittering like pirate's
jewels, a God-is-in-his-heaven wing-ding, baby, a spinning beanie of
joy"?

To read Rafael Alvarez's new anthology of short stories is to wander the streets of a swarming, dusty, gaudy, stinky town—Crabtown, by God!—and to find on almost every streetcorner the evidence for the one and only "truth" that fiction writers are ever permitted to utter: "Everything sacred must remain opaque."

Opacity!

A longtime *Baltimore Sun* reporter, Alvarez frequently refers to himself in fiction as the "Cartographer of Baltimore" (an unsteady metropolis that he also calls "The Holy Land"). And the job description seems accurate: what *are* these picaresque tales of wandering sad sacks and love-fuddled stargazers, if not "road maps" through the ineffable labyrinth, the heaped and swarming hive of our own sooty, shared Kingdom of the Patapsco?

To read an Alvarez story about Baltimore is to tumble, *a la* Alice, down the rabbit hole of the Ordinary into a fabulously polluted Wonderland where even the garbage in the alleys glitters with a mysterious halo. It's a charmed landscape down there—yet somehow familiar— on which poker-faced bluesmen croon from beneath their slanted hats and sleepy cops yawn over their java at the Sip & Bite...while the full moon rises like a fat gold bucket over the mudslop at the harbor's edge.

The Holy Land. It's the proper setting, surely, for the kinds of characters that Alvarez loves to create: dazed, feverish souls, drunk on the Infinite, in love with every form of exile, and inevitably down to their last buck.

Fumblers every one, his Crabtown drifters are nonetheless redeemed by a single gift: they tend to see life as a feast. Example: At Orlo Pound's vast and sprawling junk emporium in Canton, the rendezvous point for his trysts with the doomed Leini, the banquet never stops:

> It was fun in the beginning, the Salvage House their Hollywood wardrobe for dress-ups. They came at odd hours from different directions to meet in secret for an hour or two, ferrying kettles of pig's feet into the woods behind the bottlecap factory; making campfires in the sooty marshes of Sparrows Point, a small pot on burning sticks as the Bethlehem Steel

plant vibrated in the distance, the aroma of slow-cooked pork mixing with the stench of molten steel.

Opacity rules! Which theologian was the first to point out that "God is in the details"?

Alvarez would surely agree; in stories such as "The Fountain of Highlandtown" and "Sweet Digits of Swine" and "Johnny Wichodek's Thanksgiving Duck," his new collection endlessly celebrates the saving mystery of appearances, the immense wisdom contained in Nietzsche's famous dictum: "Everything profound loves a mask."

Another vivid example: Wandering through East Baltimore at twilight, a character in "The Fountain of Highlandtown" describes the ambiance:

> Strong Greek coffee, Delta blues, oval porcelain plates of cheese and black olives, crusty bread, cheap beer and young people from all over the world shouting at each other about what it's all about....

Or how about this pungent portrait of suppertime from a story called "Eat and Be Strong"?

> Lou lifted the lid once more and drops of condensation ran down to make a hot little puddle on the counter. He turned the food carefully and...made a ring of six clams inside the skillet's rim, made a square of four inside of that and set a triangle of three within the four.... Bringing his nose to the skillet one last time, Lou breathed in his triumph and brought the flame down as low as it would go without flickering out.

Two universal themes dominate these rousing love-poems to Baltimore: eternal salvation and food. You'll find plenty of both on almost every page, along with a wagonload of reverence for the frayed, eternally-coming-apart-at-the-seams world that is contemporary Crabtown, as a dozen of Alvarez's brightest characters struggle frantically—and comically—to sort out their tangled destinies.

Make no mistake: The ruling adjective here is "joyful." Stand on the corner of Eastern and Patterson Park Avenues...look over there, where those two seagulls are poking their beaks at that slab of discarded Burger King. Yellow-eyed, scruffy, necks bobbing in the rainy mizzle drifting in from the harbor, and there goes the No. 10 bus, lumbering along toward Dundalk....

The life we share.

The Whirli-gig!

Tom Nugent
Author, You Might As Well Dance *and* Death at Buffalo Creek
Baltimore, April, 1997

The
Fountain
of
Highlandtown

BASILIO

I LEARNED TO LIVE IN THE DARK this year when I quit my job, sold everything I owned, and moved in with my grandfather.

This new life makes the simplest things complicated, even for a guy who decides one day to quit his job, sell everything he owns and go live in the dark.

But that's my problem.

Grandpop would tell you that.

It's a fine summer night in Baltimore and I am walking from Grandpop's house to meet Katherine, who is young and beautiful and smart and almost completely unknown to me.

I haven't told her much about myself, hardly anything except that my grandmother died in the hospital where she works, that my grandfather stopped sleeping in their bed the day she passed away and that it would be better if I met her where she lives than the other way around.

I said all this last week when I found her standing in line at the Broadway Market. I was buying fresh fruit for Grandpop and she was picking up scallops and shrimp and pints of shucked oysters for a dinner party at her apartment.

Okay, she said, maybe we can do something, and borrowed a pencil to scratch her number across my bag of peaches.

And so I am walking from the little Highlandtown rowhouse where my father was born and raised, passing bakeries and record stores and coffee shops, on my way to Katherine's apartment a few miles away, up around Johns Hopkins Hospital.

It's early (I had to get out of the house) and there's still a pink wash of early evening light across the sky as I walk down Macon Street to Eastern Avenue.

The street jumps with kids on skates, Saturday shoppers coming home with carts and bundles, and heavy women squirting down the gutters.

On the Avenue, middle-aged sports with slick hair and brown shoes with white socks wait on the word; Greek men who haven't shaved for two days stand on the corners, telling lies; packs of heavy-metal kids graze for drugs and kicks and young girls walk by, dressed up for each other.

My eye swims through the center of the composition but the margins are crowded with thoughts of Katherine.

What will she wear?

What does she smell like?

What hangs on her walls?

I think: How will our time pass?

And, if things go well, will we find our way back to Macon Street? Fat chance.

My world is ruled by Grandpop and he is driving me crazy.

Right up the wall.

I am afraid that it won't last long enough for me to get everything done.

Every morning at breakfast he says the same thing: "Why are you here?"

Like he forgets that I am living with him between the time we go to bed and the time we wake up.

All night, Grandpop tosses and turns on the sofa bed downstairs, like he's being chased, until the break of day when he asks: "Why are you here?"

And then: "It's morning, turn off that light. You think I'm a millionaire? How were you raised?"

Grandpop was so poor growing up in Spain that one summer he carved an entire bicycle out of wood, wheels and all, so he would have something to ride besides an ox-drawn plow.

It doesn't matter that he's had it good in this country for sixty years, that, in his own words, he "eats like a king" and can lock the front door to a warm home he has owned for twice as long as I've been alive.

It does not matter that he's got a good pension from the shipyard and Social Security and more money in forgotten bank accounts than I have made in twenty-eight years on Earth.

None of that means shit if you are foolish enough to leave a light on in a room you have left or care to read or draw or scratch your ass by electric lamp before the sky outside has turned to pitch.

And there is no reason to use lights at night because at night you sleep.

Electricity, says Grandpop, is money. And a poor man cannot afford to waste either of them.

Bent over and angry, pointing to an offending fifteen-watt bulb, he says: "You think I'm a millionaire?"

When I try to tell him not to worry, that I'll help pay for it and it's only pennies anyway—when I smile and say, "Hey Grandpop, we got it pretty good in this country"—he says I can go live with somebody else if I want to waste money.

He asks: "Why are you here?"

But he doesn't charge me a dime to sleep in his bed and eat his food and he doesn't say a word when I do what I need to do to get my work done.

Just as long as I don't turn on any lights.

God Bless America.

God Bless Grandpop.

I cross Eastern Avenue and dart between traffic into Patterson Park, where Grandpop used to play soccer way back when with other expatriates from around the world.

It's hard for me to imagine his legs strong enough to kick a ball the length of the park; he's barely able to climb the steps in the middle of the night to make sure I'm not reading under the covers with a flashlight. But up on dusty shelves near the sofa where he lays at night and talks in his sleep like he's trying to make someone understand, there are trophies to prove it.

"Grandpop," I say. "Tell me about playing soccer in the land of baseball."

The Pagoda sits on the highest hill in the park, a surreal stack of Oriental octagons in the middle of a wide, rolling lawn; a weird obelisk of Confucius bordered all around by narrow brick rowhouses, the first in Baltimore with indoor bathrooms.

When you stand atop the Pagoda you can see all of the Holy Land, all the way past Fort McHenry to freighters in the harbor and the Francis Scott Key Bridge in the mist.

I would like to take Katherine up there and present her with the view, but it's only open on Sunday mornings when the Friends of the Park are around to let you in and keep an eye on things.

Grandmom and Grandpop used to walk me up here when I was a kid and you could go up to the top and see the whole city. They would stay down on the ground and wave up to me and I can see them now like it was yesterday, smiling through their broken English: "Doan breaka you neck."

After awhile Grandmom couldn't make the walk anymore and as I got older other things became important and I didn't care to visit Macon Street so much.

The city let the Pagoda rot while punks and drunks and whores and glue-heads got up inside of it, doing things that made the paint peel. The city tried to tear it down a few years ago when some goof on dope fell off and killed himself but the good citizens saved it and now you can only go up on Sunday mornings.

I tried to paint the Pagoda for three years before I moved in with Grandpop and I never got it right.

I stare up at it and fix its scale in my head.

I wonder: Does Katherine know any of this stuff? Does she care? Will she want to know once she knows how much I care?

What I know about Katherine you could pour into a thimble with room to spare. She is young and beautiful and smart and puts on dinner parties with scallops and shrimp.

I don't even know if she's from Baltimore.

I leave the Pagoda and walk out of the park onto Pratt Street, passing families of Lumbees and Guatemalans and black folks as the neighborhoods change the closer I get to downtown.

I hit Broadway and turn north on a wide stretch of asphalt that rises up beyond the statue of Latrobe the Architect and the derelict housing projects named in his honor; up from the harbor a good mile or two where Broadway meets Hopkins, where my grandmother died twenty years ago, leaving Grandpop all that time and how much more to lie in the dark, conserving kilowatts to save pennies he doesn't count anymore.

Katherine's apartment is in the shadow of the hospital's great dome.

The neighborhood used to be called Swampoodle before Hopkins started gobbling it up, back when Bohemians lived there, in the days when Grandpop played soccer in Patterson Park and Grandmom sat on a bench with her girlfriends and watched.

I tried to paint the Hopkins dome, too, in the last days before I moved in with Grandpop, but all I could think about was what we lost there.

I smeared the canvas with vinegar and vowed that I would not paint pictures of buildings anymore.

KATHERINE

I didn't know what to expect with this guy.

I haven't dated much lately because they've all been the same, but I said yes to this guy right in the market. I knew it would be different, but I didn't know how.

I certainly didn't expect to be picked up for our first date on foot.

He knocks on the door, comes in with a polite hello, and looks around.

Next thing out of his mouth: "I walked over because I sold my car when I moved in with my grandfather."

But he doesn't say what one has to do with the other.

He tells me that my dress reminds him of the sunflowers his grandmother used to grow in her backyard until the summer she passed away "right there," and he points through the window to the hospital.

"That exact same color," he says, staring just a little too long before telling me "it's gorgeous outside," and would I like to take a walk?

He's cute, in a funny way, like a kid; younger than me and a nice change from the clever men with tasseled loafers and Jaguars, so suave and witty until they find out I'm a doctor and then they really start acting like kids.

I don't mind walking and out we go, strolling south on Broadway toward the water.

I'd bet you a lobster that we're headed for the bars in Fells Point, where every man I've dated in this town goes sooner or later, like its the only place in Baltimore that sells beer.

But he doesn't mention Fells Point or any special restaurant or destination; he just keeps up a pleasant chatter about things you can't imagine—wooden bicycles and chestnut trees and the Rock of Gibraltar (I've seen it, he hasn't)—and now we're cutting across the side streets and through the alleys, moving east to the neighborhoods where my patients live and die.

He doesn't say what he does for a living and I wonder if it's anything at all, if maybe the good doctor is out for an evening with the unemployed. He must do something because his shoes and pants are speckled with little smudges of paint.

Maybe he's the Cartographer of Baltimore, so well he knows these cobbled paths crowded with dogs and kids and garbage cans.

"You know what I love?" he says. "I love to walk through the alleys and look in peoples' houses. Especially at night when the lights are on and the shades are up. You can look right in and see people eating and watching TV, talking to each other, you know, just living."

He doesn't ask me what I do and it's a relief not to have to answer all the questions, a blessing not to feel the evening turn when it finally comes out.

It seems enough for him just to know that I work in a hospital.

Our walk is slow and evening falls with a warm, clean breeze from the harbor.

How odd, I think, looking into the tiny concrete yards where kids splash in wading pools, moms watching from lawn chairs with their feet in the water, old men in their undershirts, listening to the Oriole game and drinking beer; how pleasantly odd not to talk about what you do for a living.

I will extend him the same courtesy for as long as it lasts.

At the end of an alley we stop in front of a corner bar called Miss Bonnie's and he points out the red and blue and green neon floating out from behind block glass in the windows.

He talks about colors as if they are alive and in between all the loose words he talks about his grandfather.

"Grandpop won't let me turn on any lights. He sits at the kitchen table all day circling crime stories in the paper with a red pencil. Nothing bad has ever happened to him here, but he says America is going to the dogs."

A Lumbee girl on a tricycle zips between us and he talks about the shades of red and brown in her cheeks, "like autumn leaves."

He says that American Indians are the only minority his grandfather has any sympathy for because there was no New World left for them when things went bad at home.

Now we're in the park, walking quietly until we reach the Pagoda, the sun going down behind it like a tangerine, that's what he says, "a big, fat tangerine."

He shakes the gate on the iron fence around the Pagoda but you don't have to shake it to see that it's locked.

"Grandpop forgets that I'm living with him between the time we go to bed and the time I come down for breakfast. Every day we start from scratch."

"So why do you stay?"

He turns from the Pagoda and we walk east across the park toward Eastern Avenue and the Greeks.

Just beyond the railroad bridge marking the incline that gives Highlandtown its name, he spies a wooden stand on the sidewalk and says: "Wanna a snowball?"

I get chocolate with marshmallow and he asks for grape, fishing out a couple of dollars from the pockets of his white jeans.

We pause at a bus stop and I wonder if maybe we're going to catch one to take us to God knows where.

Holding out his palm, he invites me to sit down and I think: This bench is the sidewalk cafe in Paris that the plastic surgeon wanted to take me to last month until he found out that a ticket to France would get me across the ocean and wouldn't get him anywhere.

We sit, the distance of five hands between us, and I look up to see that above our heads hangs one of the most bizarre landmarks in a city filled with them.

Up against the sky: the Great Bolewicki Depression Clock.

Bolted to the front of an appliance store called Bolewicki's, it has a human face and crystal hands filled with bubbling water—the little hand bubbling lavender and the big hand bubbling pink—and around it glow lights shaped into words that say: "It's not too late, it's only..."

And then you read the time.

Like right now, eating snowballs at a bus stop on a Saturday night in Baltimore, it's not too late for anything: It's only ten past seven.

"I've been to Germany and Switzerland a half-dozen times," I say, "and I've never seen a clock like this."

"It's something," he says. "I tried painting this clock for three months."

"You got hired to paint the Bolewicki clock? How many coats did it take?"

That does it!

He starts laughing and can't stop; a wild, crazy laugh from way back in his throat and I start to laugh too because he's got such a funny, genuine laugh, like some strange bird.

Tears come to his eyes and he's spewing crystals of purple ice, trying to catch his breath.

And somewhere inside of this laugh I decide that I like this man and surrender to whatever the night may bring as the No. 10 stops to let people off beneath the Great Bolewicki Depression Clock in the middle of Eastern Avenue and my date with a guy named Basilio whose tongue is the color of a ripe plum.

He gets a hold of himself and says: "I wish old man Bolewicki would let me paint his clock. It would be the first money I've made with a brush in a long time."

He looks me in the eye.

"I tried to paint a *picture* of it."

"You're an artist?"

"Yeah," he says, looking up. "This thing was so hard, Katherine. You see the water bubbling in those hands, like bubble lights at Christmas...did your tree have bubble lights when you were a kid? I loved those things, you don't see 'em anymore. But I couldn't get the water right, I couldn't make it look like it was really bubbling."

I watch as he loses himself in the clock, the big hand bubbling pink and the smaller one pumping lavender—"It's not too late, it's only..."—and he catches me looking.

"Let's go," he says.

We walk deeper into the neighborhood and he points out things I know and things I don't.

"That's a great little place," he says as we pass Garayoa's Cafe Espanol, where, he tells me, they serve squid stuffed with their own tentacles and cooked in a sauce made with the ink.

I don't tell him that I have broken bread there with an investment banker, a screen writer, and a child psychiatrist.

"The ink bubbles up in a thick dark sauce that shimmers deep green just above the surface," he says. "I tried painting with it once—thought it would be perfect for a sad night sky. But it dried ugly brown."

At the next corner, Basilio passes our empty snowball cups to a short man selling produce from the trunk of a gigantic Pontiac and in return the man hands each of us a small, brown pear.

"Lefty," says Basilio, shaking the guy's hand.

"*Señor*," says the man with a Greek accent, looking me over and winking at Basilio. "How's your old *abuelo* my friend?"

"He's good Lefty, real good," says Basilio. "I'll tell him you said hello."

"You do that, *señor*," he says. "Enjoy your evening."

We move away in silence, biting the fruit as the sky turns dark and pear juice runs along my mouth. Basilio pulls a spotless white handkerchief from his back pocket and wipes my chin, cleaning his own with the back of his hand and it is all so very simple and nice....

Until we come upon a narrow lane paved with brick and identified by stained-glass transoms as the 600 block of South Macon Street.

Basilio points down the long row of identical rowhouses, orange brick with white marble steps before each of them.

"I live down there with Grandpop," he says, pausing like someone trying to decide if they should show up unannounced at your door, making me feel like he's talking to himself and I am no longer here.

Over the next curve of the Avenue, beyond a cluster of blue and white Greek restaurants, I see the Ruth Tower rising up from the University of East Baltimore and since there seems to be no agenda and Basilio's verve faded at Macon Street, I point up to the tower where I had a blast as an undergraduate, a stone room—cool and round—with a bar and a view you can't get from two Pagodas set on top of one another.

"Up there," I say. "Let's go."

It is night now and we move through the dark campus toward a granite spiral tiled with all the great moments of the Babe's career.

It is the Bambino's only gift to the city of his birth.

Bolted to the base of the tower is a plaque quoting the slugger at the dedication: "Let the poor kids in free and name it after me."

We walk inside and start climbing, round and round, up to the sky.

I tell Basilio that when I first came to Baltimore—Good Lord, it seems like nine thousand dead teenagers ago—the top of the Ruth Tower was *the* spot: strong Greek coffee, Delta blues, oval plates of feta and black olives, crusty bread, cheap beer, and young people from around the world shouting at each other about what it's all about.

He says: "I was in the suburbs back then."

"Did you ever try to paint this?"

"Sure. Grandpop brought my old man here to see the Babe when Dad was a kid and Ruth was half-dead with termites."

We walk in and I head for the bar, reaching into the pockets of my dress for money, feeling Basilio behind me, looking around.

"So this is college," he says.

I hand him a draft beer and steer to a table with a window facing west, back toward downtown where Baltimore's money finds Baltimore's art in chic storefronts along Charles Street.

The docs I work with write big checks for paintings that probably aren't any better than the ones Basilio destroys, but I really don't know if he can paint or not. All I know is what didn't turn out: half the real estate in East Baltimore.

I sip my beer and think that maybe I can help this guy.

"Tell me about the paintings you're happy with."

He gulps his beer and ignores the question, shifting east to play tour guide again: Over there is the National Brewery, home of the One-Eyed Little Man; and the Esskay slaughterhouse is there, they've got some great stainless steel letters out front; and way over there, he says, beyond the rooftops, is a graveyard where four Chinese sailors who capsized in a 1917 hailstorm are buried.

He's a fraud, I think. And for a moment I am sick.

Turning his head with an angry finger, I direct his gaze toward the Hopkins dome.

"And over there is where I fish bullets out of fourteen-year-old boys on Saturday nights just like this before I have to tell their twenty-seven-year-old mothers they didn't make it. Take me to your work or take me home."

And still this hard-head gives me words instead of pictures.

Grandpop skinning squirrels for dinner at the stationary tubs in the basement; Grandpop lecturing a little boy at those same tubs that a man really hasn't washed up if he hasn't washed his neck; and Grandpop making love to his bride on Macon Street, conceiving the man who would seed the artist.

"Those," he says, "are pretty good."

As we take the steps two at a time, he takes my hand.

At the front door to 627 South Macon Street, just before turning the key, Basilio tells me to take off my shoes and leads me in, dim light from a streetlamp falling across a small figure sleeping in the middle room.

"Grandpop," he whispers as we creep toward a staircase along the wall.

No one answers and as I move up the stairs, the old man stirs in his bed and my dress flutters around my knees.

Basilio keeps moving and I am right behind him, shoes in my left hand and my right against the small of his back as we climb together.

When we reach the top, he whispers in my ear, his "hallelujah!" warm and sweet.

He says: "I've never done this before."

Neither have I.

A door creaks open before us as Basilio turns the knob and I slip in behind him.

We stand still in the darkness, just inside the door, and my nose stings from the turpentine. As my eyes adjust I sense that this is the biggest room in the house, that there is only one room on this floor—as long and as wide as the house itself—and I am in it.

Basilio escorts me to a saloon table against the long side wall and sits me down on a stool before crossing to the other side of the room.

"Ready?" he asks, holding a cord.

"Ready," I say, and he pulls it.

A tarp whooshes to the floor, night fills the space where the roof ought to be, the light of a nearly full moon and a sky of stars floods the room and in one clear instant I see the world this man lives in.

"There's no roof!"

My head spins as I try to take in the sky, the paintings, the smile on Basilio's face and the colors everywhere.

"I told you, Grandpop won't let me turn on any lights. I cut the roof out a little bit at a time and paint with what it gives me. I never would have thought of it if I didn't have to."

I stand, dumbfounded.

"You can't turn on the lights, but you can saw the roof out of his house?"

"He's never mentioned it. As long as I don't use electricity or bring women home, he pretty much leaves me alone."

I move close to his work, the silver light from above giving each painting a glow I've never seen in any gallery in the world and on one canvas after another I read the narrative of his grandfather's life.

Grandpop as a boy, sitting on a rocky hill, carving a pair of handle-bars from the limb of a chestnut tree; Grandpop shoveling coal on the deck of a rusty freighter, Gibraltar bearing down in the background; Grandpop kicking a soccer ball, his right leg stretched out in front of him as the ball sails across Patterson Park, the Pagoda perfect in the background; Grandpop strolling down Eastern Avenue, all dressed up with his wife on a Sunday afternoon, the Great Bolewicki Depression Clock bubbling pink and lavender to beat the band.

And then, running the length of a single wall, a huge canvas of a bedroom cast in moonlight and shadows.

In the bed is a young man who looks a lot like Basilio, a white sheet draped across his back, arms strong and taut as he hovers over a dark-haired beauty with stars in her eyes.

I am transfixed and wonder if there is a cot in the room.

"What do you call this one?"

"The Fountain of Highlandtown."

GRANDPOP

Suenos. Siempre suenos. Dulces suenos y malos suenos. Suenos de amor.
I can feel it.

Basilio must be making a *pintura* of a woman upstairs.

I can feel it in my sleep, like she is in the house.

He must be getting good.

"Grandpop," he says at my kitchen table every morning, up before me, coffee ready for his *abuelo*, this boy is a man, doesn't he have a home?

"Grandpop," he says while I'm still trying to figure out what day it is and why he is living with me.

"Grandpop, do you remember what Grandmom looked like the first time you saw her?

"What did her skin look like?"

I say: "Basilio," (he was named after me, two Basilios in one house is one Basilio too many); I say: "What are you doing, writing a book?"

"Something like that," he says.

Last week it was questions about the shipyard, before that it was Patterson Park, now it's about Mama and I don't have the patience for it.

Questions and questions and questions as he makes little pencil marks on a napkin.

"Grandpop, tell me about Galicia and the corn cribs on stilts and the baskets your father made."

"Grandpop, tell me about the ox and the cart and the *cocido* your mother stewed over the fire in the black pot."

"Grandpop, tell me about the first time you saw Gibraltar."

Why does he want to live with an old man who is so mean to him? He is good company, this boy with the questions, even if he has to turn on a light to clean the kitchen in the middle of the afternoon.

"Grandpop," he says to me on his way out of the house tonight (where he was going in the shoes with the paint on them, I don't know, he should get dressed and go out with a woman before he gets old); "Grandpop," he says: "What did Grandmom's hair look like on your wedding night?"

I told him: "Turn off the light and lock the door when you go out."

This is what I didn't tell him: It was black, Basilio, black like the coal I shoveled out of ships at *la Roca*; black like a night at sea without stars and it fell down around my shoulders when she leaned over me; *que linda Francesca, que bella Francesca, que guapa Francesca para me y solamente para mi.*

He asks in the morning while we eat our bacon and eggs; eggs he makes like I made for him when he stayed with Mama and me when he was a little boy (even then he wouldn't listen); bacon fried crisp and the eggs on top, grease spooned slow over the yolk.

I say: "Basilio, what are you doing here?"

And he answers: "What did Grandmom's eyes look like when she told you she loved you?"

And after all these years, the thought of her kiss (I can feel it at night, on nights like this, Basilio you must be painting upstairs), the thought of her still makes me excited, *un caballo fuerte*, and it makes me ready, so sad and ready, and I get mad to answer this boy with skinny brushes and silly paints and goddammit, why doesn't he go and live with his father in their big house in the suburbs?

My house is small and life here is finished.

I get mad and tell him he's too much trouble, that he's wasting my money leaving the lights on.

You don't turn on lights in the daytime and a boy doesn't ask an old man so many questions.

But he doesn't get mad back at me, he just touches my arm and gets up to wash the dishes saying: "I know, Grandpop, I know."

What does he know?

By the time I was his age I spoke good English, had three kids, a new Chevrolet and seniority down the shipyard.

What does he have?

My electricity and *no trabajo*; pennies he saves for paint (where his pennies come from I don't know, maybe he finds them in the street, he takes so many walks); and a loaf of bread he puts on the table every day before supper; one loaf of bread fresh from the Avenue in the center of my table four o'clock every day without a word.

I should go easy on him.

He's the only one who really talks with me.

The only one who comes to see his old *abuelo*.

But when did he move in?

How did that happen?

That's the question you never asked, Basilio: "Grandpop, can I live with you?"

Suenos. Dulces Suenos.

He must be painting upstairs.

I can feel it.

I remember when his father was just a baby and I called her Mama for the first time and she became Mama for all of us; *Mama de la casa* and his father would wake up in the middle of the night and scream in his crib and nothing would make him stop, *nada*, and Mama would get so exhausted she would turn her back to me and cry in her pillow.

I would smooth her hair—it was black, Basilio, as black as an olive—and I would turn on the radio (electricity, Basilio, in the middle of the night), to maybe calm the baby and listen to something besides the screaming.

Mama liked the radio, Basilio, and we listened while your father cried—*cantante negra, cantante de almas azules*—and it made us feel a little better, helped us make it through.

I had to get up early to catch the street car to the shipyard, but when the crying finally stopped sometimes the sun would be ready to pop and Mama's breathing would slow down and her shoulders would move like gentle waves, sleeping but still listening, like I can hear her now on this no good bed, and Basilio—*Mira, hombre*, I will not tell you this again—if I moved very close and kissed her shoulders, she would turn to face me and we would have to be quiet Basilio, under the music, very, very quiet....

So this I want to know, Basilio.

This, if you want to live on Macon Street for another minute.

Can you paint an apple baked soft in the oven, an apple filled with cinnamon and raisins?

Can you paint such a woman?

Are you good enough yet with those brushes that she will step out of your pictures to turn on the radio in the middle of the night?

Will she visit an old man on his death bed?

If you cannot do that, Basilio, there is no need for you to live here anymore.

Self-Portrait
No. 29

I HAVE COME TO SMITH ISLAND to fix my star within the constellation of my time.

Stand to the side, if you like, and watch.

But don't make noise and don't cross the line. I am having the best day of my life, but I'd sooner toss you to the nettles than hide in a box like Jamie up on Monhegan.

Stay on my good side, and as the image reveals itself you will have all the answers you need.

If it were only truth I was after I would parade through the streets with my head in a frame.

See the fingers emerging?

Short fingers on small hands, the hands of a woman; smaller, even than my mother's and dwarfed by the hands of my father, a good man who kept secrets and pulled wrenches in the bellies of tugboats for more than half his life.

I have spilled all my secrets, hands are scarred from madness forced down the stem of my neck; nails bitten, cuticles raw and small fists made fast to brushes the way Keith Moon held onto drumsticks and bourbon: for dear life.

Just yesterday, so very long ago, I slapped gobs of brown and maroon against broken furniture and trash can lids.

But today I could be a draftsman, so precise are the lines tracing my thumb and forefinger as they pinch a clump of backfin from the steamed carcass of a Jimmie caught this morning at the end of a twisted gray pier.

I used to think that the visions in my head could be erected without foundations, abandoning phases I never took the time to learn. Years of cutting corners nearly killed me.

Now (look, the bend in the arm brings the meat to my lips); now I do the work that no one sees because the hard way taught me that everyone can tell if you don't.

I suffered to make things happen and nothing ever did. But when I do the work, the colors choose themselves.

All of this is so fresh my brushes can hardly keep up.

I know people who say they do not think when they paint, that the work moves through them like waves and when the channel is especially clear the paint floats across the canvas like veils.

My experience has been something else: brooding and resentment forced down like an egg through a funnel; pity and self-will swelling my fingers and fraying the brushes until broken yolk drips from the canvas.

"Wait'll they get a load of me" was my battle cry.

I am waiting still, here on Smith Island with my easel before the Chesapeake to stop the clock in the time of my life.

On the picnic table with my image lies the harvest of dawn; crab after crab pulled gently from the shallow green water with chicken necks on a string, a half-bushel of Big Daddys scooped from the water with a wire net and a patience I have never known.

They say that the great ones—service being the first quality of greatness and nuance the highest level of technique—that the real heroes in this world are the ones with the courage to get out of the way.

How do you execute a self-portrait without being present for it?

How do you get out of the way of yourself?

I don't know.

Yet I am stunned by a morning that allowed me to harvest a bushel of crabs without once thinking of myself, the very thing I would coax from my palette with chicken necks of gold if the trick were so easily turned.

I am on this island to fix my image for all-time and all the world.

And I *will* taste success before I get out of the way; I am determined to turn the world on its back, crack it open like a crab and suck it dry.

Maybe then I'll let go.

I fill the margins with a soaring fig tree with scalloped green leaves as big as stingrays, leaves hiding fruit ripe and pink beneath the rind; a thicket of sunflowers on the other side, necks stretching for the sun.

How does one remain faithful to a self-portrait?

If you look in and out at the same time, won't your peepers go cock-eyed?

("Cry louder," I remember my mother saying as she spanked me for drawing on the walls. "I can't hear you.")

A narrow pier of buckled boards runs from the picnic table out to the water and at the end are crab shanties, wooden shacks where soft peelers lay in gurgling water, slowly forfeiting their armor for larger shells they will never acquire because someone will eat them first.

The shanty roofs are cluttered with crab pots made of chicken wire and beyond the bent and rusty traps lies a channel of green water whose fluid peace I seek to preserve in paint.

I could draw this island with enough detail for the cover of *National Geographic* if I wanted; rendering any shape or human form as exact as photography.

It is simply something I am able to do.

But that is factory work.

Before you stopped by I was trying to find the right shade of brown for my summer face; olive burned to bronze raked to Earth.

My face: Eyes like muddy pools of new rain above dark circles recovered from black; a long, straight nose like the descent of a funicular moving from Poland to Italy; the soft sag of a coming middle-age that I never thought I'd live to see; a mop of dark brown hair cut in the shape of a bowl since February 9, 1964.

Across the canvas, my forehead crests to the size of a dime, shrunken like a lentil and trapped in a downward glance at crabmeat clinging to its shell.

It is as close to an honest look at myself as I've managed since before I set out to reinvent myself in the sixth grade.

I used to paint myself into crowded bazaars as the Fun King, my face bloated to the size of the moon; a boy without the patience to finish an apple; circles deep and black below eyes filmed dirty yellow like the hokey man who used to sweep the gutters on Binney Street; eyes that turned from nothing on Earth.

If you think you're having fun then you are having fun and though there is little to fete in the measure of a dime it is a great success for me.

I was tempted—impatience, unpotable vapor—to crowd the canvas with celebrities and strangers and hide myself among them like poor Elvis lost in the hippie shit of Sergeant Pepper; tempted to hide as I did before every back alley and midnight basketball court in East Baltimore led me here, not all that long ago, dogs calling my name as I ran as fast as I could.

There are two piles of work back home in the basement of my little pink rowhouse in the Holy Land; a stack of canvases stretched and primed and empty and a thousand portraits of the hounds scrawled across empty pizza boxes and broken eggshells.

For years I believed that if I killed the wooing bitch I would somehow kill myself.

I bounced beer bottles off her mottled hide and ran fast but not fast enough to keep her from overtaking me, spread pig legs and unleash a litter with ten times the strength of their mother.

The Baltimore catechism couldn't kill it.

Sex and drugs and rock-and-roll couldn't kill it.

And a year of living in the dark with Grandpop only kept it at bay.

Blues fell on my palette like hail; a hard and steady pounding until, not very long ago, I lay down and waited to be devoured.

Once I'd given up, an eager pup out for his first hunt spoke for the pack: "You ain't no fun no more."

As simple as that.

(Come here, look, I have found the soft brown to color me an Aztec prince.)

The dogs ran away to chase a girl about to get her period for the first time and as I felt the weight lift, I became aware of a hole that would have to be filled soon with something good because anything might fall in to make a nest for the bitch always pregnant with plans.

I paid dearly to know this and to keep from having to pay any more I began to paint as I hadn't since I was very young.

By simply showing up at the easel every day I realized how much I didn't know.

I discovered—I don't know when, I just showed up every morning without excuse, be it my birthday or Yom Kippur—how to finish paintings I never dreamed I would begin.

I allowed the colors to choose themselves.

(Do you like the face? Could you look at it forever?)

I'll sketch in the crabs before painting their shells Halloween orange speckled with kosher salt and cracked black pepper; bay green armor turned fire red by a blue flame beneath a stainless steel pot.

(Go over to the table and finish up what's left. I can catch more.)

When the beautiful swimmers had reduced my chicken necks to tatters, I took a link of my brother's homemade chorizo from my lunch, threaded a line through the marbled meat and watched an inlet of crabs dance through clean, shallow water to taste it.

When they hooked their pincers and nibbled with lust, I scooped them up with smooth and quiet sweeps of the net.

The bushel grew fat but wasn't quite full and when the sausage was gone, I pulled a live crab from the basket, held my foot on its back, and cracked it open like a spade cutting into a field, its flippers spinning in death as I halved the carcass, hooked it on a line and waited.

The cannibals went in with the others: contentious crabs of green and white and a blue you can't get from a tube if you squeezed the sky at both ends.

I cooked them on a Chambers range in the white-shingled house where I am staying, eating a few for breakfast before hauling the rest down to the docks with my easel.

Now they are fixed for all-time amidst anonymous blossoms and a portrait of the artist drawn to the size of a dime.

The table is done, my arms are done, my shirt, sunflowers, figs and crabs—all done; the rickety pier and the shanties at its end in a contentment all their own.

Perhaps I will build a frame from scraps lying around the island, bits of traps, splinters of shanties and crab shells bleached in the sun; perhaps it will hang here alone, no greater gallery in the world; here for the watermen and their families to contemplate on Sabbath afternoons with the knowledge that Prayer Changes Things, my eyes turned away.

Only the water is left to do, water surrounding everything on this low-profile oasis between the tidewaters of Maryland and Virginia.

Such a different story from a year ago, when the easel wobbled down at the end of Clinton Street, the canvas blank so I could project my never-ending movie upon it.

If you happened to be struggling with a portrait of your own I would have persuaded you to set the brushes down and join me in the klieg lights.

If you were married I would have said: "Where is he now?"

And if you were tired I'd dip down into my pocket and promise that a little bit of this will surely take care of that.

Here on Smith Island it is hard for me to believe that this rippling peace flows from the same source as the water at the end of Clinton Street a hundred miles north where dogs shit in their water bowls.

Old-timers say there was a day on the Baltimore waterfront when you could catch a bushel of crabs wherever the harbor met the shore, when Big Jimmies nearly crawled up on land and the bounty was so plentiful that gin mills used to set bowls of steamed crabs on the bar just to keep the stevedores drinking.

Just yesterday, so very long ago.

The Great Chesapeake springs fresh in Pennsylvania and makes its way down to Baltimore and its port of legend.

The water runs out from the harbor basin and on through Curtis Bay and rivers called Magothy, Choptank, and Nanticoke; on down to the Big Annemessex and the Straits of Kedges just beyond my gaze, all the way to the Unhooped Oceans of the Earth.

I am a single drop from it all, happy to have traveled from there to here and, with daybreak, back again to home and the Right Side of a Good Thing.

(Come, look...

I am done.)

Johnny Wichodek's Thanksgiving Duck

BY THE TIME THANKSGIVING was upon Baltimore in 1962, Johnny Wichodek had half-a-load on, a long night of work ahead, and a strong taste for the sweet blood of a duck.

He had a hankering for *czarnina*.

Johnny worked on the tugboats that docked at the Recreation Pier where Broadway meets Thames Street; a neighborhood deckhand who was full of himself when he was sober and full of everything else when he wasn't.

And when Johnny got a big idea in his head—like how sweet a Thanksgiving it would be to slaughter a duck on a bobbing tug in the middle of the night—no one could stand him.

"Ain'tcha sick of turkey all the time—turkey, turkey, turkey. Every year turkey. So dry," said Johnny to the engineer as they killed time on the stern. "We could have us a nice duck, ain't it Chief? A nice, fat Muscovy."

"You're goofy, John," said the engineer as the Resolute waited for orders to move a sugar ship from the Domino berths across the channel. "Where the hell you gonna get a duck?"

It was a little past eleven on Thanksgiving eve and one last job stood between the crew and their holiday.

The job at the sugar house would surely take the men to the other side of midnight, pushing the holiday OT clock into triple-time, wages that would afford Johnny with enough cash in one half-hour to buy a pond of ducks.

Big paper, but the idea in his head was bigger.

He was going to put on a feast they'd be talking about on the waterfront for years; ached to see his friends wipe pear and blood sauce from the corners of their mouth, belch, and marvel: "I thought them days was gone."

At the moment, with them days gone just about everywhere but the inside of Johnny Wichodek's pickled noodle, a late November moon dressed the harbor in pearl.

The lights of barges and buoys trimmed it in red and green and the 113x67-foot reflection of the Domino Sugar sign shimmering across the Patapsco carpeted the water in orange neon.

The air was crisp.

The sky clear.

It felt like Thanksgiving.

Johnny and the Chief gazed over to the sugar docks where bucket cranes dipped into the belly of the Domino Crystal, scraping her bottom for the last grains of brown sand to be polished into table sugar, a moving belt of shadows high above the white lights of the ship.

The Chief was serene, ten years older than Johnny and as different from him as tugs are from skipjacks. In olive green coveralls, he sipped black coffee laced with Anis del Mono, the gift of a Spanish crew from Vigo the Resolute had handled earlier in the week.

Johnny had been drinking beer since early afternoon, his sweet duckling dreams the only thing between him and a sullen drunk; too worked-up to be thankful for what he had.

"The way my grandmother made 'chi-nina'—outta this world Chief," he said. "It was our big meal every Sunday after Mass, every Sunday we could get a duck."

"Chinina?"

"Duck blood soup," said Johnny. "Something special."

"Right."

"You bought the duck and the blood came separate in a jar," said Johnny. "Some people make it on the sour side, but my Booshie liked hers sweet, with prunes and brown sugar and a nice pear sliced up.

"I can see 'em in that alley house on Binney Street, Pop out back with his fist around the bird's beak, talkin' soft and comin' up slow with a straight razor—zzzzip!—clean 'cross the top of the head. I wasn't allowed to watch, said it would give me nightmares, but you could look straight into the yard from the back bedroom upstairs. Geez-oh-whiz, Chief, compared to the shit you see when you're growed up, watching my grandfather knife a duck ain't hardly nothing. He'd bleed 'em in a bowl until they passed out."

"You ever done this, John?"

"Seen it done a million times," said Johnny. "After Pop died, Uncle Vaju tried it in the stationary tubs downstairs. Said there'd be less mess, wouldn't let nobody help. What a racket! We heard all kind of squawking and cussing coming up through the floor.

"Vaju runs out the basement door white as a sheet, making a beeline for his favorite stool over Aggie Silk's and this duck is flapping around bleeding on the walls and don't drop dead for an hour. Hey, you gotta know what you're doing."

"I'm sure," said the engineer, smiling over the top of his mug.

"The old ones knew," said Johnny. "Pop would hang the duck upside down from the doorknob in the kitchen to get every drop. How much blood you think you get from a duck, Chief?"

"How much, John?"

"You get a cup, you get a lot. Once you got it all, you dip the bird in scalding water and pick the feathers for pillows. Years back, everybody did it. Them old Polacks were like the Indians with the buffalo. Nothing went to waste."

Way, way, way, back.

Johnny stared across the water to the Domino sign and in the middle of the mammoth "D"—high above the endless loop of rolling buckets—a grown man saw a little boy who loved to watch his grandparents cook.

Johnny sipped his beer and as if the Chief was no longer there, began to recite the Apostles' Creed.

"A little vinegar went in so the blood wouldn't curdle, that was the big worry, 'cause you could chuck it all if it did. When Pop was done dressing the bird, Boosh would cut it up and drop it in a pot of hot water, skimming the fat. She'd set the meat on the side just before it was falling off the bone and run the broth through a strainer, covering the bottom of a roasting pan with it. In with the broth went a chopped onion, a bay leaf, a little more vinegar and then..."

"What then?"

"Huh?"

"What then, John?"

"The blood."

Maroon mercury in a mayonnaise jar.

"Booshie'd pour it in the pan, stir in a half-dozen spoons of flour and whip it up good, real smooth," said Johnny, warmed by the memory of how the flour lightened the color of the blood.

"A little more vinegar, extra broth and then you add your meat. Boosh simbered all this together forty, maybe forty-five minutes, adding some sugar if it was too sour, more flour if it was too loose, picking out the bones. Then the rest of the broth went in with the prunes and pears last, not too soon or they'd melt on you."

"Your grandmother wrote this down?"

"Got it all up here," said Johnny, tapping his temple with his beer can, getting his biggest smile of the day from the Chief.

"I was Booshie's taster, front row seat, no taller than the stove. She'd ladle some out and I'd taste it a half-dozen times while it was bubbling. Wasn't done 'til little Johnny said it was done. Delicious, Chief. And noodles! Homemade egg noodles! How could I forget the noodles?"

"How could you forget the noodles, John?"

"You make 'em from scratch, you know, eggs cracked inside a circle of flour, beat 'em up with a fork like the dagos do. Oh man! Chinina with them good noodles. Why shouldn't we treat ourselves, Chief? Huh? It's Thanksgiving. Tell me why we shouldn't."

With Wednesday about to become Thursday and the bucket cranes across the channel hardly slowing down, the engineer tossed the grounds at the bottom of his coffee cup overboard and said: "Wise up, Ace. Where the hell are you gonna get a duck at this hour?"

Johnny threw his beer can over his shoulder and jumped onto the pier.

"SMUTEK'S!" he yelled.

Johnny crossed Thames, hit the corner at Ann Street, swung around the mailbox in front of Zeppie's Tavern, and raced two blocks up to the poultry shop that kept Slavic Baltimore in fresh chicken, duck, turkey, squab for the finicky, and goose on certain holidays.

Johnny hit the alley just before Fleet Street, stopped on a dime and crept in behind Smutek's, which was protected by a high brick wall and a wire gate with a heavy chain around it.

Kneeling down, like a kid staring through a banister on Christmas Eve as his parents set out the presents, Johnny gazed through the gate at birds stacked in wooden coops, a pig on a leash tied to the clothesline, and a tree stump in the middle of the concrete yard as wide and flat as a carving table.

All was quiet, the animals asleep; but as Johnny stood to find his way inside, the back door swung open and a fat woman with a kerchief on her head and an ax in her hand came down the white wooden steps, mumbling in Polish.

Johnny dropped to his stomach and peered through the wire at Old Lady Smutek, the bird butcher of Broadway with the hands of a stevedore.

The moon glinted off the blade of an ax, an edge so sharp it split the silver light as the old woman muttered an old country chant of idiot children: "Yiddal, yiddal, yiddal, bah, pah, mah..."

In English, she complained: "Gobble, gobble, gobble."

Whoever had ordered this stupid bird should have done it a lot sooner; whoever it was would pay a pretty penny now.

A pretty penny, thought Johnny, watching her grab a turkey from a coop near the ground, the yard suddenly alive with squawks and grunts of birds whose number would come up sooner than later.

"Getting me out of bed in the middle of the night with Thanksgiving tomorrow and all I got to do," said Smutek, holding the bird between heavy knees and stretching its neck across the splintered stump.

"Turkey," she bitched as the ax came down. "So dry."

The gobbler's head flew off into the darkness and Johnny swallowed hard, the words of the Chief ringing in his ears, the cold ground numbing his ribs.

"Ever done this John?"

Mrs. Smutek hung the turkey upside down from a hook in the bricks and the blood began dripping onto the concrete, a dark, thin stream heading Johnny's way.

How would he bleed a duck on a moving tug?

Nobody would lift a finger to help him.

The pig began lapping the blood as the butcher laid her ax on the stump before going inside.

Johnny got up from the ground, listened hard to see if the buckets were still moving at the sugar house, and, hearing only the pounding of his heart, told himself: "You seen it done a million times."

When he vaulted the gate, his right shoe came down in a sticky pool of blood.

He squinted into the dark coops to make sure the bird he grabbed was a duck, grabbed one that looked good and set a $10 bill under the head of the ax.

Dropping the coop over the gate as gently as possible, he saw the lights come on inside of Smutek's and followed the coop over the side.

The cage cracked when it hit the ground and by the time Johnny reached it, the duck was squirming its way out. Down at the Recreation Pier the Resolute's captain was blasting a special cadence of whistles he used every time Johnny Wichodek said he'd be right back.

Down below, the Chief fired the engines and spoke beneath the diesel roar: "Come on John, move your ass..."

Pulling the duck from the busted coop, Johnny couldn't resist dabbing a finger in the turkey blood rolling toward the sewer grate in the alley.

With the duck under his arm, he set his finger against the moon with the delight of a school boy who'd just placed first in the science fair, thrilled at how the dark treacle conducted energy.

Finally hearing the tug's whistles, Johnny kicked the coop out of his way and raced back to Thames Street with Old Lady Smutek yelling "thief!" on her back steps.

The Resolute's whistles blew with an urgency nearly equal to Johnny's taste for czarnina, yet he stole three minutes to rush into Zeppie's for a victory shot of Old Crow.

"Put it on my tab, Marion," he told the barkeep. "And if you're a good boy I'll come by tomorrow and treat you to a nice bowl of chinina."

* * *

Between the time Johnny jumped ashore and the moment he finagled his heart's desire, the buckets had stopped moving at the sugar house.

Wheels were turning on the Resolute and if Johnny didn't hurry, they would turn without him.

The tug was pulling away from the pier as he raced across Thames Street and he bounded aboard like an athlete running the high hurdles.

"Go to hell," said the captain, sticking his head out of the wheelhouse.

"Yez-us," said a deckhand doing his work and Johnny's too.

"Chief," he barked into the hole: "Chief, you gotta see this."

Popping out of the engine room, he marveled: "The goof got a duck."

"Ain't it!" crowed Johnny, holding the frightened animal high above his head, dancing a jig on the stern as brown water churned beneath the Resolute. "The goof got a duck."

Johnny ignored the hawser lines being coiled fore and aft as the tug moved toward Locust Point and Domino Sugars.

He was tickled with himself and thankful, finally thankful as midnight delivered Thanksgiving to Baltimore and the Resolute made its way for the Domino Crystal.

How sweet it is!

He could taste it.

When the Resolute sidled up to her mark, Filipino deckhands waiting to take lines from the tug spied the brown and white duck under Wichodek's arm.

Crowding the rail, they pointed down and jabbered with great excitement.

Johnny didn't understand what they were saying but he knew what they wanted. He tightened his grip on his prize, looked up at the sailors and cackled: "Eat your hearts out!"

With the bird plump and warm under his arm, he started for the middle of the boat and the sharpest knife in the galley but as he turned, the wake from a passing tanker banged the Resolute against the Domino Crystal.

The drunken feet that had spirited Johnny over the cobblestones of Thames Street and launched him over Smutek's wall faltered on the cold steel deck and as he fell backward—his ass landing in a coil of rope, his ears stinging with Filipino laughter—Johnny Wichodek felt his misfortune fanned by a flapping of wings.

He stretched out his arms, but they only reached as far as his fingertips.

Gupjak.

Pijak.

Goof.

Rubbing his eyes, Johnny saw his grandmother at the stove on Binney Street as his duck cut a frantic swath through the harbor sky; his dreams soaring, one neon letter at a time, across the length of the Domino Sugar sign, free and in flight for Curtis Bay, the blind sanctuaries of the Chesapeake and the vast wetlands of the Eastern Shore.

The Daddy-O
Dance Party

ON DECEMBER THE 14TH OF 1980, Yoko Ono requested of the world an ocean of silence in which to remember her beloved.

I was twenty-four, wed but a week and unaware that I was pregnant for the first and only time.

It was a Sunday and the silence arrived as I stood at the stove in the basement of my mother-in-law's house, making Italian waffle cookies for Christmas: thin wafers of gold flavored with anise and formed by squeezing dough between the scored jaws of a searing hot iron.

I held the iron over a blue flame, waiting for my husband's mother to drop the dough before pressing down with a quick "Glory Be to the Father," turning the iron and saying the prayer to myself again.

When I opened, she'd pluck the confection free with a fork, lay the cookie on a table covered with waxed paper and drop more dough.

Rock-and-roll meant nothing to this woman yet during the appointed time she never said a word and the only sound that passed between us was the banging of the iron and pizzelles dropping gently.

The daughter that was born to me is grown now and her father has not been my husband for a very long time.

But in that silent winter's afternoon, I'd wondered why I felt so weak, didn't know why I missed my mother and remembered this story.

* * *

Mom took a job on a party boat called "My Way" when I was eight years old and she was gone a lot.

Dad didn't mind having to take care of us, that was pie for him 'cause he was a kid himself. The part he didn't like was Mom cooking and entertaining for a bunch of businessmen and politicians who were always calling up and saying they needed her.

Daddy didn't like the way she wouldn't come home and he didn't like the way she did.

I know he didn't because we didn't.

It wasn't too often at first, but little by little they started calling all the time at all hours and she'd drop everything and leave our little Highlandtown rowhouse in tight, straight skirts and sequined blouses; shiny nylons and high heels, her frosted hair sculpted like icing on a cake, wrapped tight way up on top of her head.

One Sunday morning she left while Dad was still sleeping and us kids ate cereal and watched cartoons. When she walked down the stairs it looked like she was stepping off the cover of one of those "For The Secret Loves of Secret Lovers" albums by Jackie Gleason or somebody.

"Awww Mommy," cried Joanie, the baby. "Not again."

"Shush," said Mom. "You'll wake your father. Tell him I'll call later."

Joanie's whine brought Dad down the steps in his boxer shorts and he caught up to Mom in our little vestibule. He closed the door, but I could see their silhouettes through the beveled glass, early Sunday sunshine shooting between their stiff bodies.

Dad grabbed Mom by the elbow. "Christ Shirl. What's going on? I haven't seen you in a week."

"Don't start John," she said, jerking away. "Don't start with me."

And then she was gone, high heels clicking against our white marble steps like nail heads.

Daddy walked back in like bad milk had gone up his nose; pulling his hair back from his forehead with lines crinkling down around his eyes, like he didn't even know if he was awake or not.

It was almost Easter, 1964, and the Beatles had six songs in the Top Ten.

"TV off," he said. "In the kitchen. Family meeting."

"How can we have a family meeting without Mom?" asked Petey, who was almost two years younger than me.

The last time Dad called a family meeting was to say it was getting too expensive to keep our membership down the shore and before that was when I almost didn't make my First Communion because I couldn't memorize all the rules and the nuns said I spent too much time listening to records and not enough time studying my catechism.

Joanie and Petey ran into the kitchen and plopped down in their chairs, plastic bowls speckled with dull milk and soggy Lucky Charms still on the table.

Dad nudged me forward: "You too, missie."

He poured himself a cold cup of coffee from the pot Mom had made hours before, the radio on top of the refrigerator still tuned to the Sunday morning polka hour.

Dad sat down, sighed, and took a moment to look at each of us: Petey wide-eyed with his arms flat on the table; Joanie's bottom lip quivering and me staring right at him.

"What Daddy?"

"Well kids," he said and instead of talking he took a deep breath and scratched his ear.

And while his mouth was open in a lop-sided circle—right before he could say whatever it was he was going to say—the polkas vanished, a crazy DJ shouted "AND HERE THEY ARE!" and a golden weave of guitars washed over us like a wave; the drums and guitars and happy shouts like a fresh breeze pushing everything out the screen door.

I squealed.

It was *them*.

"Can't buy me lo-ove, everybody tells me so, can't buy me lo-ove, no-no-no...NO!!!"

Daddy listened for a moment, like he was hearing them for the first time even though you couldn't turn on the oven back then without hearing them and his head started moving from side-to-side, a funny little smile on his face like the one Petey got when something fascinated him that nobody else could see.

"Kids," he said. "Is this a great day for a party or what?"

"Hoooraay!!!" yelled Petey, standing on his chair.

"Yippeeee!!!" screamed Joanie.

"Daddy! Daddy! Daddy!" I shouted and he lifted me from my seat.

And as we twirled around the room, my eye caught a glimpse of the old Philco on top of the fridge and my heart marveled that such magic could come from a brown plastic box.

Dad cleaned the house and made a million phone calls. He let me invite anyone I wanted and their parents too and when he took up the rug in the front room to scrub the wooden floor it was the first time I'd ever seen him on his hands and knees.

I was in charge of giving the little ones baths and dressing them for the fun—"Wear anything you want," he said—while Dad went out to shop for the party.

Just before popping out the door, he said: "If your mother calls, tell her she's welcome."

He came home two hours later with a mess of ground beef, hot dogs, fresh rolls from the Greeks on Eastern Avenue, six cut-up chickens, soda, pretzels, three cases of National Bohemian beer, and a sack of stuff he wouldn't let us see.

"Mom call?"

"Nope."

He put the beer in a washtub of ice in our narrow backyard and dug a hole between a pair of rosebushes near the alley, filling it with sticks and charcoal before laying a huge grate from a factory fan over top of it. When all of the neighbors were buying fancy rotisserie grills, mobile things with shiny hoods and hubcaps on their wheels, Dad came home with this grate and told Mom it was our new barbecue.

"Oh John."

Dad was always bringing Mom weird things from his "travels," stuff he said nobody could get anyplace at any price, gifts Mom never found a use for.

If she didn't give the stuff to us to play with and break, it'd wind up in the room at the end of the hall upstairs where we put things we never used: screens with holes in them, clothes that didn't fit, bowls for fish that died, leashes for dogs that ran away; all jumbled together around a bed with one leg shorter than the others so it always felt like you were falling off if you tried to sleep on it.

The phone rang and rang after Dad put the word out—I think he invited everybody he knew and everyone he ran into while he was shopping—and between rings he reached a man we knew as Uncle Leo.

"Lee, it's me again," he said, pacing in little circles and twisting up the phone cord. "My hi-fi is shot, Shirley says its already ruined all of her Sinatra records. Can you bring your portable and some of that new stuff that moves? No Al Martino. Great. See ya soon."

And then he went upstairs to shower and dress and put me in charge.

No one came for a while and the house was quiet except for Dad making noise upstairs. It seemed like he was up there forever and it sounded like he was moving furniture; drawers opening and closing as he paced up and down the hall a hundred times, grunting until I finally heard the door to the bathroom close and the shower run.

Uncle Leo backed his way in the front door with a big black box with a hard plastic handle, set it on the coffee table against a wall in the front room, told Petey not to fool with it and ran back out to his car, a sporty Italian job that Mom always liked but said a family could never fit in even if we could afford one.

That's why she went to work, so we could afford things.

Uncle Leo was even younger than Dad and he came back in with a crate packed with record albums, a thousand bands with funny names that made Joanie and Petey giggle when he read them out loud.

"Dig this cats and jammers—it's time to meet those four little boys with bangs—THE BEATLES!!!"

I gave out a shriek and Uncle Leo tousled my hair, shouting: "England's newest hit-makers, the ROLLING STONES!, the ANIMALS, HERMAN'S HERMITS, PAUL REVERE AND THE RAIDERS! ("the British are coming! the British are coming!" he cried, holding up the Beatles again); Gerry and the PACEMAKERS, the KINKS!, and the ZOMBIES!"

Petey's favorite was the TURTLES. He laughed and pointed to a fat guy on the cover with glasses and crazy hair and Joanie kept saying over and over "Hoor Mins-Hoor Mitz," bouncing on the floor to the rhythm it made.

I liked most of the groups and listened all the time to the transistor radio I got when I finally made Communion, but I loved only the Beatles. Mom called them the Cockroaches and said they were stupid and crude.

Like she was the weatherman or something she predicted that I'd be asking for Barbie dolls again by Christmas.

One night after she started working she came home late with her earrings in her hand and peeked in my room to see if I was sleeping. I liked it when she came in to talk late at night, but this time the first thing she saw a brand new poster of Ringo taped over my bed.

"Look at that mutt," she said, walking out. "What kind of name is Ringo for a man?"

When she leaned down to kiss me her breath was sweet and sour at the same time and I sang "I Feel Fine" real loud in my head but I couldn't turn it up loud enough not to hear Daddy whisper: "Christ Shirley, it's 3:30 in the morning and you're bombed. What kind of goddam job is this?"

"Relax John," said Mom and Daddy punched the wall and said: "I wish that fucking boat would sink."

Mom was always on the boat.

Uncle Leo gathered up the albums and said: "Okay kids, these goodies are for later. Let's get the fire started for your old man. Petey you be my helper. Girls, shape some burgers out of the ground beef."

"OKAY!!!"

The radio on top of the fridge was still on and Uncle Leo fiddled around with it until he found the station from the college up on the hill. Music spilled out of the Philco that I'd never heard before and I was sure there wasn't any of it squeezed in with the fun in his crate.

I couldn't figure out why anyone would listen to it: lonely, squealing notes from guitars that sounded like they only had two strings, like somebody was skinning baby cats with razors while ghosts stood around and cried.

Dad yelled down for Uncle Leo to turn it up.

A few of his friends showed up with their wives and kids and potato salad, one of them with his fist around the neck of a full bottle of whiskey. Then came a bunch of kids from the neighborhood, led by Cindy, my best-friend and co-president of our Beatles club. She showed up with her little brother and their babysitter who went to the college on the hill and the party started to hop.

The kids ran around with Joanie and Petey, climbing on the furniture and scrambling under the legs of the grown-ups who filled our pink and green rowhouse with food, booze, cigarette smoke, and gossip.

"She says she's a hostess on a yacht," said one lady, who didn't know I was listening. "Can you imagine?"

"Poor John."

Uncle Leo put some burgers on top the fan screen with a dozen hot dogs and one of the chickens and the grill began to sizzle and hiss as fat dripped to the fire in the hole.

"Works better than that fancy-pants job we bought down 'Monkey' Wards," said a man staring down at the screen.

"Perfect," said his wife, bending over in lavender pedal-pushers to grab a beer from the tub.

Cindy and I were walking through the party to look at Uncle Leo's records when I felt footsteps on the stairs and looked up to see Daddy. He stopped and spread his arms wide.

"What do you think, Sweetie?"

I couldn't believe it.

He looked like the cover of a record album. He'd shaved and his face glowed fresh and pink. He had on polished black penny-loafers without socks, a purple turtleneck, bleached white jeans...

And his pompadour was gone!

The wispy curls that Mom always nagged him to trim dipped over his ears and straight black bangs ran from one side of his forehead to the other, just above his eyebrows.

I jumped up to hug him.

"Daddy! You're a Beatle!"

"Neato!" said Cindy, whose father wore a crewcut.

Her babysitter stuck her fingers in her mouth and whistled like a boy and Dad's friends clapped with cigarettes clenched tight between their teeth, squinting with smoke in their eyes.

"Va-va-va-voom!" said one of the wives.

Dad waved from the banister and took my hand, whispering: "Baby doll, your old man is a cool rockin' Daddy-O!"

"Mom oughta see you now!"

People crowded around Dad like he'd just gotten off a plane, asking questions and grabbing at him. Women kissed his cheeks and men slapped him on the back. Somebody handed Dad a beer and he made a joke, laughed and pushed his way through the crowd to the back yard, holding my hand.

Uncle Leo was telling a story to a pretty lady and when Dad put his arm around him they looked like brothers.

"So they land at O'Hare and the reporters are peeing themselves, climbing over each other trying to keep up and Paul asks this TV guy if he knows where they can hear Muddy Waters and the suit says: 'Who's Muddy Waters?' Paul cocks that one eyebrow and says: 'Don't you Americans know who your own famous people are?'"

Dad and Uncle Leo laughed like that was the funniest thing they'd ever heard but the lady just looked dumb and said: "Who's Muddy Waters?"

"Set up the box Lee," said Dad. "Let's shoot the moon."

Uncle Leo edged back into the house with people spilling into every room and crowding the hallways, standing with paper plates and drinks, talking loud and laughing.

Daddy collected the children around him and took us downstairs to the summer kitchen where we crowded around a long table. I could hear people banging around in the yucky bathroom in the back near the stationary tubs and washing machine. The door was latched from the inside and you could hear giggles between squeaks and muffled noise, like somebody bumping into something over and over.

Dad grabbed a tray of construction paper, kids scissors, glue and crayons from the top of our old china closet and said: "This just ain't any party is it, kids?"

"NO!!!"

"No indeedy. This, my little moon doggies is a DADDY-O SUPER ROCK DANCE PARTY CONTEST!!!

"YAAAAY!!!"

"A contest with PRIZES!!!"

"YAAAAY!!!"

"Now here's whatcha gotta do," he said, taking a piece of pink paper and a pair of scissors. "Before we can give out prizes we need categories," and he sliced a circle, made a yellow tail and glued them together like a ribbon. "This is an award. To get a prize you must earn an award."

Daddy leaned over the table with a crayon and wrote "Most Like An Angel" on the ribbon and held it up.

"Whatsit say, whatsit say?" cried Joanie.

"Most like an angel," said a kid who could read.

"That's me, that's me," said Joanie.

"You know it sweetie," said Dad. "But once the dancing starts the judges decide. I want you guys to make a couple dozen awards, anything you want."

"Like first place?"

"No," he said, a little strict. "Not first or second or runner-up. Just like I showed you."

"Most Like Mister Ed?" asked Cindy's little brother.

"Bingo!" said Dad. "Like that. Anything but winners and losers."

And then he ran upstairs.

In less than an hour, while the adults moved their heavy feet across the floor above our heads, we had more than fifty awards: "Most Like An Astronaut," "The White Tornado," "Twistin' Like An Egg Beater," on and on and on.

Cindy and I did most of the printing for the little kids and while we were putting on the finishing touches, her babysitter and some man came out of the bathroom with their eyes red like marbles.

The babysitter got excited when she saw what we were doing and asked if she could help. The man arched his back and went upstairs without looking at us.

The babysitter's award was all curves and fringe. In the middle of the circle she wrote—half-printing, half-cursive—"Most Like A Poet" and stuck it inside her shirt before she ran upstairs too.

"She's weird Cin," I said.

"Yeah," she said. "She scares my brother."

We put all of the awards in a bowl except for "Most Like An Angel," which I slipped into my pocket when no one was looking. I carried the bowl upstairs with Cindy right behind me and the kids following us.

"Okay Dad," I said, handing him the bowl. "Ready."

He set the awards on the kitchen table with the desserts, picked up a butter knife and clanked it against a beer bottle, shouting: "Okay you good people. Everybody in the front room!"

He and Uncle Leo put chairs in a half-circle between the middle room and the front room and Dad stood on one and announced: "Welcome to the Daddy-O Dance Party of 1964! It's a simple game. Either you dance or you judge. If you don't dance you gotta judge and if you judge you gotta wear a hat...and...

"ALL KIDS GOTTA DANCE!!!"

A half-dozen people with excuses decided to judge—some said they'd eaten too much, some claimed their muscles hurt from working in the yard, and two or three said they never danced and never would.

Dad gave each of them something to wear from the days when he used to try and get Mom to play dress-ups with him: an Orioles' cap; a ranger hat; a ten-gallon cowboy job; a combat helmet; an Untouchables fedora; and a tall, puffy chef's hat.

The judge's sat down and Dad passed out pencils and scrap paper so they could take notes. Uncle Leo opened up the record player and spread its wings. He pulled the first album from the crate, slipped it from its cover, and pushed the vinyl down over the spindle.

Uncle Leo turned a knob on the box as far as it would go and in a blink the house was swimming in music; bodies twisting and turning, hips shakin', heads boppin', and feet kicking across the floor.

"I don't wanna kiss or hold you tight...I just wanna dance with you all night..."

The album cover was sitting on the sill of our big front window and when I danced in front of it, I was sure it was throbbing: four dreams singing their hearts out under a marquee of ten thousand lights that spelled: SOMETHING NEW.

It even seemed like the furniture and the pictures on the wall were moving.

Dad had Petey on his back, Joanie riding his right leg, a beer in one hand and me holding tight to the other as he hopped around the floor, talking to everybody, swigging beer and shaking his head.

When the Fab Four put their mops together and screamed, he kicked his loafers into the hallway.

"My dogs can breathe!" he cried, wiggling his toes. "My dogs are free!"

He bopped to the center of the room, us clinging to him no matter how fast the music went, and Cindy's babysitter led the other kids in a ring-around-the-rosie outside of us, dancing in one direction while Uncle Leo got the adults to make a bigger circle going the other way.

Two grown-ups wiggled a made-up dance and I heard the man shout in the woman's ear: "Ever since February these guys have owned the radio, but I never actually thought of dancing to it, I mean, it's always just been noise to me. My kids play it night and day and I'm always screaming at them to turn it down, but you know something? This is the easiest thing I've ever done."

The woman smiled with her eyes closed and the house rocked from one song to the next, even during the blank spots between songs, the room a blur.

Round and round and round we go....

Cindy screamed that it was better than any ten birthday parties she'd ever been to and I shook my head up and down when all of a sudden the beat changed and a lot of dancers left to get drinks and fan themselves while some of the married couples stayed on the floor to slow dance.

"...treasure these few words while we're together...keep all my love forever..."

Sweat dripped into Daddy's eyes from the pointy tips of his bangs as he walked off the floor with his hand on Petey's head; the sun dropping in the window behind him like a big tangerine when Cindy's babysitter broke through the crowd, grabbed his free hand and made him dance.

Her shirt was half unbuttoned and drenched from the wild dancing and you could see a thin black strap from her bra hanging off a wet shoulder as she led Daddy back out to the floor.

I'd thought she was weird before but now I thought she was weird and stupid, and I stood stiff and mad against the wall, wishing it was Mom out there dancing with Dad to any kind of music.

Pulling his face back from the babysitter, Dad said: "You go to college on the hill, don't you?"

"I do. I see your wife leaving for work all the time too. I guess that's where she's going, all dolled up like Viva Las Vegas."

She was the first grownup I ever wanted to hit.

"And then she doesn't come home for hours. I bet not until after you and the kids have already eaten dinner."

Dad got like he got once in awhile after he'd been patient for too long. He pulled the girl's arms from his waist and said: "What are you studying up there, newspaper work?"

The babysitter took the sweaty "Most Like A Poet" award from inside of her shirt, held it in front of Dad's eyes and shoved it in the back pocket of his jeans and he left her dancing out there by herself and stood with me against the wall to be near him until the song was over.

"I miss Mom," I said and he said it was time to give out the prizes.

All the kids got 45-rpm records and crayons and tiny little notebooks and a bunch of other neat things that Dad pulled from the secret sack he'd brought home.

Cindy's babysitter traded her prize—a can of sardines for being judged "Fresh As Live Bait"—for a notebook from a kid who said his grandfather loved canned fish. Then she sat in a corner by herself and scribbled.

The adults got things like unbreakable combs, small jars of hand cream, and plastic salt and pepper shakers with Chinese people painted on the sides. Dad said the party was prize enough for him.

Everybody left saying what a fabulous time they'd had, like they really meant it, and a few leaned in close to Dad on the way out and said they hoped everything turned out all right and that they knew it would because things always do.

The babysitter tried to kiss Dad when she left with Cindy and her little brother but he turned away and in my head I gave her an award: "Most Like A Turd."

Uncle Leo stayed behind to help clean up and a couple of the older neighborhood ladies told Dad to call if he ever needed anything.

"Anything at all," they said.

As they were going down the front steps, I heard one of them say: "Did you see that young girl hanging all over that poor man? Mooshie-ocking like some kind of vamp with his wife out trying to make an honest buck. It's that goddam rock-and-roll. Mark my words, Treesey, it ain't no good."

When everyone had gone except Uncle Leo, Dad went out to the backyard, took off his shirt and ran the hose over his head. He pulled his brand-new bangs back from his face, looked around like he could see again, and squirted water onto the dying embers in the hole beneath the screen. It was getting late.

"Hang around awhile willya Lee?" he said, coming back inside. "Sit and have a cold one while I straighten up."

"Sure John. I'm with you."

I helped Petey and Joanie change into their pajamas and when I tried to get into Mom and Dad's room for a brush to comb out Joanie's hair, the door was locked. I got them into bed and started back downstairs when I saw an award taped to the door of the junkroom at the end of the hall: "Most Like A Ghost."

I went up to get a better look and the door fell open and I saw all of Mom's stuff just thrown inside: her clothes and jewelry, her vanity, her pillow.

My heart dropped into my stomach and I couldn't breathe. All the hot dogs and soda and cake I'd had began moving around and I ran downstairs as fast as I could, trying not to throw-up. I was too scared to tell Daddy what I saw and asked instead if I could listen to some of Uncle Leo's records.

"Keep it low," he said.

Uncle Leo squeezed my shoulder and said: "You know how to work it, don'tcha big girl?"

I went into the front room and sat down on the floor next to the record player and even though I was sick I wanted to stuff myself with all the music in the crate.

The needle dropped and John and Paul began singing to me and only me, George was giving me guitar lessons in my room and Ringo was on his way to pick me up at school on a motor scooter.

Just beneath the beat I could hear Dad and Uncle Leo talking in the kitchen and when I forced myself to look up I saw all the way through the house to where they sat and my ears flew to their lips on wings.

"You don't know for sure John," said Uncle Leo. "Give her the benefit."

"I know," said Dad, taking the "Most Like A Poet" award out of his back pocket and tossing it on the table. "And as sick as it makes me, it's more than that. It's that and more and I'm wore out from fighting it."

"So what are you gonna do?"

I turned down the sound and squeezed my eyes tight waiting for Daddy to answer. When he did, John and Paul stepped back from their microphones, George packed up his guitar and Ringo ditched the scooter.

I was stuck in the back of a dark, smelly basement with Mick and Keith.

"Have you seen your mother, baby, standing in the shadows?"

Mom made it home hours later, fumbling with her keys, her heels spiking the stairs. I'd cried myself out but my stomach still hurt. Nobody was awake but me and I heard her take her shoes off in the hall and spend ten minutes in the bathroom, running water and humming a pretty tune until she tried to get into her bedroom.

"John," she whispered. "John, open the door."

I got up and looked out the door to see Mom jiggle the knob a few more times and try to pick the lock with one of her hairpins.

"You son of a bitch," she said and when she started to turn around I jumped back in bed, pretending to sleep when she came and stood in my doorway. I peeked out from under my eyelashes as she stared around at all the pictures on my walls in the light that came in from the street.

I think she was crying.

"Yeah, yeah, yeah," she said. "Those goddam cockroaches."

And I turned in the bed so there wasn't room for anyone else but me.

PIG FEET AND MUDDY WATER

*The
Orlo and Leini
Stories*

Sweet Digits
of
Swine

A HALF-CENTURY AFTER HE FOUND LOVE nibbling pig knuckles down at the end of Clinton Street, what remained of Orlo Pound lay in a candy tin the fabled scavenger had rescued from the furnace of a Patterson Park rowhouse.

Leini sat in the front row of mourners, eyes fixed on the Baltimore Clipper hammered into the tin, a rake cutting the sea.

In the requested moment of silence—moments for which you are not taught what to think adding up to more than an hour of your life; a kind word worth one coin and silence worth two—Leini thought of pig's feet and Orlo thought of her.

The first five dollar gold piece the junkman found on the sidewalk he could not tell you. And he forgot every priceless vase hauled out of some biddy's parlor the moment he turned it over.

But to this day, a pile of ashes in a can made for caramel cremes, Orlo remembers every mote of dust that passed through the fading sunlight at Ralph's Lunch the first time he saw Leini Leftafkis with her nose in a book.

No matter that it took fifty-two years—from June 28, 1926, to November 10, 1978—for her to be seen with him in any way that could not be construed as coincidental.

She was sixty-nine now, Little Leini at her side in a metal folding chair at the Salvage House; her daughter unmarried and pushing thirty—eyes too close together, perhaps too far apart—the same age as Orlo when the junkman asked her mother for a second helping at Ralph's.

Presiding was the Reverend Shane, the Unitarian preacher who lusted for the cathedral radios Orlo found so easily, who years ago, upon receipt of a particularly fine wireless, had humored the lovers by pretending to marry them despite Leini's husband.

It's only dress-ups, Leini told him.

Make believe, said Orlo.

Shane, a brilliant man with more humor than faith, knew they were more married in their hearts than most who'd said "I do" in the Church.

"If there is a royalty among herbs, Madeleine reigns sovereign," he eulogized. "No other is so revered for its beauty, fragrance, symbol, and use...in Spain it is the pilgrim blossom and children believe that fairy babies sleep in its flowers and swing from its branches...where Madeleine flourishes, the woman rules..."

Orlo listened and knew he would love Leini through the end of this world and the one to come; one of the privileges afforded by death: no doubt.

He knew it the way scientists at Johns Hopkins were certain— *almost certain*—that the storing of memory involves chemical changes in the nerve cells of the brain.

The way nothing—*almost nothing*—triggers memory more strongly than the scent of simmering food wafting through an open window.

From pig's feet to porridge, there are thousands upon thousands of smells in this world and no two people receive them exactly the same way.

How does memory solidify?

The way pig's feet jellies in a pickling tub.

And the garbage cuts—feet and jowls, head, ears, and tail; desired by the discerning and plenty for the poor—sit on top of spaghetti, all covered with cheese.

Love.

How do we form the handful of memories that accompany us to the grave?

Through the marriage of repetition and intense emotion.

"Please stand," said Shane, walking the urn over to Leini and leading the mourners out into the nickel afternoon; Little Leini helping her mother with the load as the parade trailed down the pier jutting out from the Salvage House to the harbor.

Balls Maggio walked a bicycle hung with his special ball-snatcher and strict orders not to try and fish anything out of the water; the eighteen-year-old Basilio Boullosa, sad and stoned behind perfectly round shades, had cut religion class at Transfiguration High to come, wondering where, now that Orlo was gone, he'd find the gigantic frames for his rock-and-roll landscapes.

(You will make them yourself, thought Orlo.)

Mr. Diz arrived with a fist full of upside down smiley-face balloons; Jimmy Jackson, the huge hearted sport who gave Orlo tickets to ballgames for each lacrosse stick the junkman found and restrung, carried Novenas for an agnostic; William Donald Schaefer paid respects to an old friendship based on a single question—"How can we keep good people from leaving the city?"—and Pio Talle traveled from his jewelry store at Eastern and Bouldin to thank Orlo for heirlooms discarded by thoughtless heirs.

Bonnie Sabotka hauled a pocketbook full of vidalia onions and tears she brought for Orlo but shed instead for a King gone now more than a year as Virginia Baker lumbered down the pier with a box of jumping frogs.

At the last minute, *The Sun* dispatched Jay Spry from the rewrite desk to fetch six paragraphs, two quotes, and a picture of the dead.

(Spry's editors decided to hold the obit when seven flakes of snow fell on Calvert Street and all other news lost its urgency. A week later, the *East Baltimore Guide* put Orlo's funeral on the front page.)

"See Eddie" Lichtenberg passed out "Orlo Lives!" t-shirts he'd screened in a back room of Shocket's the night before; the poet David "Foot Long" Franks stuck a microphone in front of everyone he passed and Dantini the Magnificent refused to perform or speak.

Good-hearted souls who knew of Orlo's great secret and never said a word; the people he met in his travels—"I got my feelers out for you..."—and those who traveled to meet him.

All there.

David "Hosebag" Klein, too cool in a pair of canary bell-bottoms, burned off rolls of black and white film with a camera that only worked in Baltimore and only then on certain streets.

H. Jefferson Knapp came dressed as Lincoln, a case of Scotch liberated from the High Step on his shoulder and Miss Fronie Lukowski took a day off from her floor scrubbing to say goodbye.

Even Ruthie not yet born and the grandparents Lulu will never have were there.

Characters without end, for this is Baltimore.

At the pier's end, Shane said a few more words he wasn't sure he believed and everyone stood still as Leini moved to the edge, a brisk wind blowing the hem of the same black dress she'd worn for twenty years: heavy veins and black knit stockings below purple knees.

She shook Orlo's ashes into the Patapsco like a gardener spreading mulch, licked her thumb and traced it around the crevices of the tin.

With nothing left, she licked her thumb again, passed the tin to Little Leini and took an orange from the folds of her dress, peeling it as though there were all the time in the world.

(There is.)

Holding a ragged piece of rind close to her face, Leini squeezed it to see the spray, a bit of magic unknown to Dantini that Orlo had shown her one day in the hope that it would be as real to her as a honeymoon.

Leini tossed the peel in after the ashes and followed it with her Class of 1926 ring from Patterson Park High School, a Baltimore Clipper ship cruising through the blue stone.

And then she slipped a piece of orange in her mouth and turned for home, the crowd parting to let her pass as the wind swept Orlo Pound's ashes across the water and Mr. Olie, an old oiler from the engine rooms of Oslo, took a half-pint from the pocket of his butterscotch sport coat, took a belt, and yodeled across the channel:

"I like-a you, you like-a me...?"

* * *

They met on Goose Hill, three miles east of Monkey Row and as far south of Patterson Park as you can go without getting wet.

Ralph's Lunch on one side of Clinton Street.

The Salvage House on the other.

On a humid week night in June of 1926—about a month after Leini graduated third in her class behind the son of a Jewish grocer and the daughter of a German one—Orlo stopped in at Ralph's for a plate of hot food and the glass of beer that marked the end of his daily wanderings.

As he threw a tarp over the day's haul, a small breeze swept beneath the humidity, drying the sweat on his neck moments before he finally spoke to the girl about whom he'd heard so much.

More, finally, than a glimpse of her arms sunk in dish water or the wisp of a blue skirt turning a corner.

She sat against the wall in the last booth before the kitchen; following a gang of Americans not much older than herself as they drank and lied their way through Paris and Spain; waiting for Miss Ralph or her husband to give her something to do when all they wanted was to see her and know she was safe, making good on what they'd promised her family back home.

The book was new, borrowed from the Goose Hill branch of the Enoch Pratt Free Library; its spine bending for the first time as Leini waited for something to happen in a newly matriculated life where the local library, her guardians' lunchroom, and the Greek Orthodox chapel on Ponca Street were the only places she could go without a chaperone; as frustrated as the Ralphs were happy to see this child of Hellos at her leisure, reading English as good or better than most anyone they knew who was born here.

(Escape masquerading as leisure and the ability to read English better than anyone born along the Baltimore waterfront not quite the feat they imagined.)

Leini's left hand bare for now.

Just now and just barely.

The wet hens thusly yoked—the Greeks who'd arrived before Leini; the feather-plucking Esthers along Lombard Street and the filial failures on the silk road of Park Avenue as well as the bluest bloods among old Baltimore's debutantes—all swore that affection grows and one day you no longer despised your husband's shaving mug, his elbows, or his spoon.

One day, they told the virgins, you wake up in love.

No one would ever see any Greek in Orlo—it wasn't to be found in the great-great-grandson of limey shipbuilders who'd settled Fells Point before the Revolution—but you couldn't help but see the good in him.

The cow bell on the front door of Ralph's clanged sometime between seven and eight and brought Leini back from San Sebastian to the foot of Clinton Street; a bookworm beauty tired of saving nickels for trips she couldn't take, using her tongue to do what her brain could not—sort out the gristle from the meat.

Ralph's pig's feet were the best on the waterfront, absolutely the best. Even the grave-diggers up from Carolina said so.

Fat trotters of gelatinous pork butchered fresh on Goose Hill; a plain meal, stewed except when boned and stuffed and served with simple sauces—thick purees of apples and pears—recipes so old they echoed an age when meat needed help to be palatable.

At Ralph's they brushed their pig's feet with melted lard and rolled them in bread crumbs and fennel before slipping them under the broiler.

But at least once a week—today—Mr. Ralph made them the way Leini liked best: marinated in a caper vinaigrette and simmered in a thin broth of tomato and basil.

When Leini looked up from her meal, a man about whom stories were told was coming her way.

Sometimes, she'd heard, he wandered all the way down to the strawberry patches of Anne Arundel county.

"Some pie Leini?" asked Miss Ralph, passing by on her way to greet Orlo.

"No thank you," said Leini, eyes on the door as she pushed a pebble of cartilage out of her mouth, wiped her fingers, and turned the page.

Orlo took a seat cattycorner from her and took a good look—short hair, black as olives, pale skin and an innocent neck—before the teenager dropped into her book.

(Knowing that a twenty-nine-year-old blue-eyed junkman with the chisel of Britain in his chin was not the way to go should have been as easy for Leini as Miss Ralph's pie; indeed, resisting Orlo would have spared her an impulsively arranged marriage.)

"Hello Orlo," said Miss Ralph, setting down his beer, hand on her hip. "How is life in the world of junk?"

Leini came up for the answer and Orlo caught her in the window between Miss Ralph's hip and the crook of her arm.

"People still throwing away fortunes," he said. "This morning I found one of Mark Twain's typewriters."

"Thisavros," smiled Miss Ralph, who didn't know Mark Twain from Mark Trail and whose fondness for Orlo would put her a half-step behind the story. "What can we get for you, Mr. Lucky Man?"

"The pig's feet look good."

Leini blushed from her armpits to her scalp, closed the book, and sat up.

Mark Twain's typewriter!

Hadn't she cut her hair in a bob without asking anyone's permission?

Taken to using "chap" and "rather" with her girlfriends?

Started scratching out a novel at the little saloon table next to her bed?

"I'll get it," she said, surprising herself and Miss Ralph, who walked away to cash out the register, calling out: "Dig down good, Leini. There's just a little left on the bottom."

"That's the beauty part," said Orlo, watching Leini walk to the kitchen, black shoes and white socks below a bow of apron strings, and nudge Mr. Ralph out of the way to ladle out the last of the day's special.

She came back with a bowl like her own, piled high and steaming and set it down at the empty place across from her, pulse racing but spoon steady as she resumed her meal.

"Tell me," she said, "about Mark Twain's typewriter."

(We can trust him, thought Miss Ralph as Orlo settled into the chair across from the teenager; an old woman admiring a young woman's verve, staring down the counter to the back of the junkman's curly blonde head; Mr. Ralph at the stationary tubs in the back, deep inside the pot from which the last of the pig's feet had come.)

Orlo pointed to Leini's book with his fork.

"You know it?" she asked, not knowing anyone who did.

What didn't Orlo know—basement cleaner, alley creeper, and attic sweeper with a freedom so far beyond the typical working man as to be understood only by derelicts and carnival men, searching for goodies in the rags he baled for the Schmata Kings of New York, carting off only the things that had been let go of first.

(The beauty part.)

Arriving late to estate sales, after the vultures who circled the obits had made off with jewelry and furniture—the easy stuff—Orlo would bargain the doors off the hinges and the stained glass transoms above them.

His wanderings would falter in the weeks after he met Leini and for months he could not shake the picture of her pulling string that held pig knuckles together through the space between her front teeth.

Soon, they began to find a way to share a crock of pig's feet cooked as no one had ever cooked them, the scavenging of junk license enough to be anywhere at anytime as Leini learned the hard way that it was a hundred times easier to slip a drunken husband than the good intentions of Mr. Ralph and his wife.

Insane, clandestine love.

Ralph's burned to the ground a week after Leini's wedding party took place under a blue and white tent behind the lunch room; pigs wandering the periphery of Leini's feast but not the menu.

And while Orlo had been invited as a guest of Mr. Ralph, he chose to watch his lover's leap from the roof of the Salvage House; the same spot where he sat and watched the firemen a week later; our lives made up of could have beens *not* should have beens and nothing determined but fate transparent as tissue paper against the sun.

While conflicting accounts survive, Mr. Ralph and his wife did not for very long, crippled by the fire that destroyed their business and buried with the knowledge that Leini had never been tricked by anyone but themselves.

As Orlo and Leini talked through their first meal together, a loose kid named Girlie Schuefel from up the street sauntered in with a parrot on her shoulder to fetch dinner for her family.

"How 'bout some of them good feet, Miss R.?

The parrot squawked as Miss Ralph turned up her palms and said: "We just sold out."

*   *   *

Who told you they ate pig's feet every time?

It mattered, but it didn't matter most.

Sometimes they'd throw in a tail for a treat.

Or sat on Orlo's pier to share an orange as the sun set, the junkman holding it against the sky to compare orbs before Leini peeled it with the nail of her thumb.

Sometimes they didn't eat and barely spoke.

*   *   *

"It's not too late," chimed the Great Bolewicki Depression Clock. "It's only the Last Supper of Orlo and Leini."

The junkman's turn.

Leini got off the bus for the long walk down south toward the water and the derelict sprawl of a house with one simple word white-washed across its side and bleached down to shadows on the shingles: SALVAGE.

By the fall of 1978, Orlo's home was the only building on Goose Hill still standing from the old days. For years its doors had not flown open for the grand market of fleas that had brought generations—from the flappers to the freaks—down to the end of Clinton Street.

Even the library was gone, the readers gone to television and the suburbs.

It had been so much easier for Orlo and Leini to keep their secret in the past twenty years, since life as they understood it began unraveling when Leini's husband fired a gun into his mouth on November 22, 1963, in sympathy not for America but private dramas that Leini knew from the back of his hand.

Easier since the people who knew them began moving away and dying and folks cared less about who came and went from where.

Easier, but not half the fun. Now they could walk the streets holding hands if they wanted; two old people too old for anyone to notice or care.

Aside from the spinsters who fed wild cats, half the people who wandered to the crumbling seawall were lost in their own affairs and the others—ship spotters and kite flyers—took Orlo and Leini for siblings who'd never broken the family spell.

Once a week—*to this very day*—they met, with less drama and none of the costumes or intrigue; simply for comfort and company and pig's feet.

(Theirs was the longest running, undetected love affair in the history of the western world: insane, clandestine love from the moment when falling into the deepest hole on Earth was not on the list of things to do that day.)

Does Earth plug a hole in heaven?

Or heaven plug a hole in Earth?

Leini took steady steps, walking without a cane and turning her back to the street when trucks rumbled by: loud, dirty monsters that in one lifetime had replaced ships and trains as the way to move cargo in the United States.

"There goes Old Lady Leini," said a teenager in an AC/DC t-shirt, riding a skateboard with a girl balancing on what was left of the curb. "My grandmother says she and the junkman have been doing it since Babe Ruth was in reform school."

"So?" said the girl, admiring Leini's shoes.

"So everybody knows. Her mental husband caught them in the bathtub and blew his brains out. Orlo and Leini are the oldest story on the Hill."

"So good for them," said the girl, running off into a sharp wind that chilled Leini through her coat as she rapped against the Salvage House.

Orlo kissed her dry lips and hung her coat on the horns of a billy goat inside the door, another denizen of Clinton Street survived by Orlo's junk and little else.

Everything he owned belonged to someone else before it belonged to him.

The chairs he sat in, the bed he slept in, the pots he cooked in.

Back when he kept fish, the bowl they swam in.

"Something smells good," said Leini, moving toward the kitchen. "Something I've smelled before?"

"How would you know if you hadn't?" he said.

(Tiny receptors, like the transistor radios on which Orlo made a fortune in the early 1960s (you can still see mental patients walking down Pratt Street with them, radios the size of a sandwich in jackets of perforated leather); receptors deep in the nose bond to gas molecules to send signals to the olfactory bulb; the bulb's nerves threading minute holes in a bony plate to trip circuits in a part of the brain where precise firing patterns—meatloaf in the shape of a rectangle and pig's feet a spinning top—reveal to the rest of the brain what smells so good.

Or not so.

Smell is keenest in childhood, followed by a long leveling that lasts through late middle age before dropping off the table after sixty-five to produce an eighty-one-year-old man with only half the smell of a girl taking in the fragrance of adventure for the first time, its bouquet by-passing consciousness.)

Leini stepped through Orlo's junk with a practiced grace.

"Little Leini wants to help you straighten up," she said. "She thinks you'd be a rich man if you knew what you've got."

"You see what I got," said Orlo.

Leini stopped at a small vanity, one thin drawer on each side and curved wings of leaded milk glass attached to an oval mirror.

Its finish had been blonde, turned black now from a sticky lacquer that'd settled over the house in Orlo's refusal to cover his frying pan when he cooked no matter how Leini scolded him.

On the vanity lay a piece she'd never seen, a wooden box with a map of the Holy Land carved in the lid—coordinates that once reached damn near to Pennsylvania reduced now to a thin blue band around the harbor rim, growing smaller with every rape and murder, soon to cover a shrinking acre of junk at the end of Clinton Street.

Leini lifted the lid, panpipes began to play and her mind gave words to the melody the way Helen Keller's fingers traced pictures for her mind.

She heard a recipe for pig's feet: the Ballad of Orlo and Leini, the wooden map no larger than a decorated candy tin.

"Let's eat," she said.

(All this useless beauty: so much had come to Orlo in his time that he'd taken to tossing it into the stove with the firewood; not when it was especially cold, just because he felt like it.)

Orlo put a stew pot on a cutting board between them, next to a round loaf of bread and with a ladle he'd recovered from the rubble of Ralph's—cleaning it up and forging a new handle—he scooped out a pair of fatty knuckles dripping with a thin red sauce of tomato and basil.

He served Leini and then himself, struggling to tear the bread with his hands before Leini did it for him, making him mad before he sat down and raised a glass of cold water.

"To you," he said. "Who makes me new every week."

"Every other week," said Leini.

Years of such weeks. They had come together on playgrounds, beaches, and rooftops, by the side of the road and in open fields; blankets doubling as tablecloth and bed sheet.

They'd made fires where none had burned since the meteor showers, cooking their delicacy in combinations no one had ever tried. That's what is left in the end, the struggle: Sweet digits of swine melting in the blood of ducks, pots of black ink from squid, and—on bright, cold winter days—bobbing through tureens of clear consommé.

Orlo prepared none of these today.

In a corner of his stone basement, where he used to can peaches and fresh tomatoes and steam bushels of crabs, working on new concoctions between visits with Leini and trying them out on surrogate palates, Orlo kept a bank of oak filing cabinets City Hall had unloaded after World War II.

The cabinets were fat with envelopes, old bags, and scraps of paper covered in the scrawl of five languages, two of them dead; chicken scratch detailing sauces dreamed up to seduce the long-seduced; recipes from newspapers and housewives and the memories of itinerant cooks who passed through joints like Corrales on the west side of Broadway, Winterling's on Foster Avenue, and Aggie Silk's in the shadow of two can companies and a packing house.

Recipes spilled out of hat boxes and orange crates, jumbled together with experiments from the tips of their tongues.

On top of the first cabinet sat a dirt-choked typewriter that Twain had never seen but on which Leini had pecked out three half-baked novels before telling Orlo to get rid of it.

Shelves lined a wall across from the cabinets and on them Orlo would let fruit age until the moment before ripe turned to rot—red and black currants, pears for cooking with honey, and rows of melons; shelves littered now with dried seed, all that was left of aromas so pungent that Orlo believed if he started again from the beginning he might live long enough to make it to the middle of the pile.

Fifty-two times fifty-two.

There are hardly that many recipes for fish, much less pig's feet.

On a third wall: round sandstone jars for keeping salt pork.

Early this morning, Orlo removed one of the lids and washed off a half dozen pig's feet before rubbing them with crushed bay leaf.

Leini pulled the string holding these same knuckles together, moved it between her cracked lips and let the thread glide across her tongue.

"Something new?"

"Have we ever repeated?"

Leini could turn two eggs and a piece of cheese into a meal for six—*la Cuisine de Misere*—a lifetime of singing the "Come In My Kitchen Blues" had taught her to make meals not from anything, but nothing: peeling fresh walnuts from Druid Hill Park until her fingers turned yellow, meals that cost no more than the effort it took to bend down and pick them up.

"Something old," said Orlo.

"I know this sauce."

"You asking or telling?"

(If you couldn't ignore most of the smells and even the lightest touches of this world, you would never get anything done.)

"It's Ralph's," said Orlo. "I made him recite it to me after the fire. I make it for myself when I can't see you."

Leini's own kitchen on Ponca Street was sterile, efficiently American and nothing more, for in the secret feast of Orlo and Leini there was no such thing as a moderate oven.

"But I'm here," she said, reaching for the hand of a man who'd be dead of bad valves and pig fat within the week. "I'm right here."

* * *

Leini had never been chased by the bulls of Pamplona, taken a midnight ride through the streets of Paris, or even gone back to Greece when her mother and father passed away.

The excitement of finding something no one else thought to keep was as close as she'd gotten to the books she loved and it was not lost on her that the author who'd beguiled her youth—a tough guy who presumed to know how every story turned out—had blown his head off like another drunkard she knew while Helen Keller had died like an angel in her sleep.

With the mourners behind her and Orlo above her, Leini bit deep into her orange and let the juice run down her chin, the wind making it dry and scratchy, more so when she wiped it with the sleeve of her coat, wondering how long it would be before she joined Orlo when a red tug with a white dot on its stack came near, the Resolute with Ace Gentile at the wheel.

For years, the Ace had treated the lovers to long and aimless rides, down to the Curtis Bay water tank and back—just long enough—places intelligent husbands could not find with both hands and a map.

He did so, like so many of Orlo and Leini's protectors, not just because he was fond of Orlo but out of envy for the junkman's story, because he got something from being near to it.

Remember that time?

Who could forget?

We talk about it to this day.

Leini turned toward the water as the Ace blew a whistling farewell, a black wreath on its bow, an empty barge in tow.

Muddy
Water

"For to His angels he has given command about you; that they guard you in all your ways. Upon their hands they shall bear you up, lest you dash your foot against a stone..."

—The 91st Psalm

This is George's story and he would take it back if he could.

Even I couldn't help him this time.

I had strict orders: Let him go.

On the Fourth of July in 1948—across a long weekend in which Orlo and Leini had again run off to make love and eat pig's feet cooked as no one had ever cooked them before; when the great Muddy Waters traveled to Baltimore to sing the blues in the basement of a Chinese laundry on Eastern Avenue—on this fine day, George Thanos was losing the last part of his mind that worked.

George was under my wing and I had to let him go.

(Either you believe or you don't. It is not your doubt that makes us real and our constituency is what disbelievers would expect—little kids, drunkards, grade school nuns, and goody-two-shoes.

Sometimes we take turns with especially hard nuts and on this day I drew George.)

The Fourth fell on a Sunday, the night the Muddy Waters Blues Band was booked at Spiro's Downbeat, a fat blue thumb throbbing

77

amidst fish stalls, bakeries, tubs of olives, and tanks of squid in a neighborhood where people raised children not to act like Americans.

Just two days before, Leini told George another wonderful lie; Orlo hired a boy to look after the horse that pulled his wagon, and the lovers disappeared with a weekend's change of clothes, a bag of lemons, and two dozen salted trotters between them on a steamer headed down the Chesapeake.

Leaving George alone with reason.

Reason enough to hire a half-dozen busted onions to spin the shimmy-shimm-koko-bop in the middle of the night as he drank alone and played with himself in the Downbeat; thinking and trying not to think.

George was many things—itinerant seamen, petty thief, hopeless drunk, and whore monger—but he wasn't responsible for his wife's long affair.

And while his maladies always made it easy for Leini to sneak away when he chose the Downbeat over home, the sea over home, or a bottle at their son's grave over home; George tried to ignore what he couldn't prove.

What I could not tell him is that his spooks would sprout like the dandelions Orlo and Leini picked for garnish if he buried a knife in the junkman's neck or emptied a pistol into his wife's drawers as he'd savored for so long.

Just back-handing her wasn't getting it anymore.

Before dawn, after George had finished brooding and couldn't jerk off anymore, he slipped each of the dancers a bottle of Downbeat booze, paid them out of petty cash Spiro used to fence stolen saxophones and shepherded his chorus line into cabs headed west out of the Holy Land.

And then he passed out, naked except for white socks and brown shoes, cursing through spittle in the corners of his mouth when Spiro found him the next day; nine o'clock in the morning on the Fourth of July.

Spiro stood behind his right-hand man—his flunky, his bunky, his baby, his boy—holding George's trousers before his partner's bloated face, an empty wallet dragging them down in the back.

"I know it," gurgled George in his stupor. "Like it crawled up my ass and died."

"Take it easy," said Spiro, draping the pants over George's back and fetching him a glass of water, biting his lip and wondering what kind of parade George had marshaled and what they had stolen.

Wishing they'd taken George with them.

Still, he was grateful for the chance to forgive his old friend such nights, more and more of these nights; glad for another opportunity to absolve himself for the cover he afforded George's wife and her beloved junkman.

So much talk going around for so many years.

"Oh yeah," said the Polish widows. "They been doing it since Babe Ruth was in reform school."

Spiro bore Orlo no ill, this American with the gift for finding treasure in the debris of other people's lives. The junkman brought Spiro boxes of records most people didn't know existed, giving the Downbeat the best colored jukebox between Richmond and Harlem.

No one in Maryland had a copy of Muddy's "I Can't Be Satisfied."

The day it was released in Chicago it sold out before the sun went down, yet here in Baltimore, Spiro had two: one for the box and one for his collection.

For this and other favors the crafty Greek paid Orlo well.

With a wink he told the junkman: "I see nothing."

Without one, he told George the same thing.

Spiro put a glass of fizzing Bromo Seltzer under George's nose.

"Easy, friend," he whispered, kneading George's pale shoulders as morning light fell across the black and white tiles on the floor.

"This is a big night for us. How big no one knows. The great Muddy Waters is coming here, to my club... Let me tell you about this man, this giant."

Not again, thought George, unable to remember the face of a single woman from the night before; Leini's lies too good for him, lies mixed up with too much truth.

George's hangover told him to go out and find them today and kill them both.

He missed his wife and had to shit so bad he was afraid of messing the chair.

Spiro pulled up close to George and said: "Seven years ago, Alan Lomax decides he will be the one to find Robert Johnson, but Robert is already gone, killed dead Georgie—poisoned by a jealous husband..."

"Please!" cried George.

"But Mr. Lomax didn't know. He went down to Mississippi from the Library of Congress with a record machine in a suitcase to search for a dead man. You should visit Mississippi George—out in the fields it is almost as beautiful as Greece, seas of green across the Earth and you'd be surprised how many of our people have restaurants there. Robert Johnson cannot be found above the ground but does not give up and the people tell him: "Robert's gone, but there's someone else...""

Spiro brought his face close to the odors pouring off of George's face.

"He finds the great Muddy Waters riding on a tractor!"

George's body moved to constrict but it was too soggy.

Sluts on his skin.

Leini gone.

And Spiro lording the blues.

"Please," begged George, pulling at puffs of flesh under his eyes, his bowels rumbling.

Spiro stood and spread his arms toward the low stage where a few hours ago a half-dozen naked women had stuck their tongues down each other's throats.

"Tonight..." he declared. "This same Muddy Waters will sing the blues here on Eastern Avenue and people will come from all over because Spiro Alatzas has told them it is a thing not to be missed."

(Holy Christ, thought George, he thinks he's FDR.)

"The boys from the papers will be here; radio, too. The word went out. Pig-Eye the prize fighter and even Billie is on the list, Miss Holiday herself, and I need you George, tonight of all nights, to clean up and pull yourself together."

George lifted his head from the table and stared sideways at his boss, skimming what little fuel was left in the compost heap burning inside him.

"And every one-armed, wall-eyed, *skilo-mavros* loving freak in Baltimore," he said, his guts narrowing with each hateful word until he jumped from the table and ran naked to stationary tubs at the back of the club, screams muffled in nausea.

George vomited into the tubs, his bowels exploding with liquor and grease.

"Who gives a fuck?" he raged, the words bouncing between the smooth concrete walls of the tub and his ringing ears.

"For what?" George cried, near tears, his body smeared with filth, not enough orifices on his person to drain everything that wanted out. "To hear a bunch of street-sweepers with marbles in their mouths? Everybody makes their own trouble."

George heaved and wiped his mouth with the back of his hand.

"The fucking blues," he panted. "You're the only one who cares about that noise. Everybody on the block hates us for bringing the coloreds in and half your customers show up just to see if somebody's going to get stabbed."

George turned the spigot full on his head, the water hammering the back of his neck, the spray cool on his face as it bounced off the sink, which he soon plugged up and let fill.

He soaked his head for five minutes, only coming up for air, plunging down again before Spiro could start preaching.

Under the water, he heard his mother's voice.

"When you were a baby you drank from a bottle, got sick, and messed your pants...and still you drink from a bottle, get sick, and mess your pants..."

George came up shaking like a dog.

"You stink," said Spiro, dumping a bucket of trash from George's party into a trash barrel near the back door, a thick cascade of stale beer, soiled panties, cigarette butts, busted condoms, and chewed food. "You talk dirty and you stink."

Spiro left and George opened the faucet on a claw-footed bathtub against the wall, hot water this time, diarrhea running down the back of his legs and into his shoes.

He lowered himself to the water and rested his head on the back of the tub, water spilling over the side as he tried to sink below his problems.

A bigger junk collector there never was.

Nothing salvaged.

And no one gave a fuck.

He'd said so himself.

The sun forced its way through block glass above George's head and dappled his body so it looked like he had a skin disease, a leper bathing in sewage.

Getting out, George walked around the club for his clothes, dripping puddles. He buttoned a soiled shirt around his wet chest and forced trousers over soaked shoes, tearing out the cuffs.

Holding onto the walls, he made his way behind the bar and took a pint of vodka from a shelf and an empty beer pitcher from the sink, filling it with cold water.

He walked back to the mop room, edged his way around the stinking trash barrel and stumbled out into the back yard where the rising heat of day smacked him with a promise to burn.

His Jimmy dead almost three years now, killed at Normandy.

(Thank you America, said the French.)

Leini suspected she was pregnant but didn't want to believe it, not sure whose child it would be since George sometimes took her by force. At thirty-nine, she was as weakened from her escapes as her husband was from his.

And the junkman's pony had another long weekend in the feed bag.

George squeezed into a thin shadow under the eaves; his back scraping against the bricks as he slid down with the pitcher in his hand, the last cool vapors of dawn passing from the bricks and into the pores of his back, his last comfort of the day.

The sun turned the alley into a sea of broken mirrors. George cupped his eyes to squint into tiny yards where women in black squirted down the concrete, the heat bearing down through the oily swirl of his beached pompadour.

But the sun could not penetrate his skull.

Not like George wanted.

It didn't melt his brain so the old ladies could squirt it down the alley and into the sewer grate where boys fished out rubber balls with coat hangers.

George pushed the pain into his temples with his thumbs and un-buttoned his shirt, a golden Orthodox cross poking through thick hair on his chest, the sun hitting it just so, sending out shards of light.

(George was largely a bad man—more bad than good by now—and I'm always amazed at how many men like him wear religious jew-elry. By itself—without supplication—it never helps.)

Turning his face to the sun, eyelids crimson, he mumbled a prayer no God would embrace: "Just help me find them together."

When he tried to think of Leini with affection he saw instead the copper-assed girl who had bobbed before him a few hours before, rocking between his knees on a low stool, hands clasped behind her head.

Maybe the sun will bleach it away, he thought, like horse bones in the desert.

Maybe Leini will lose her taste for pork.

Maybe I should just go home.

Muddy Waters was coming to Baltimore to sing the blues at a Greek nightclub in the basement of a Chinese Laundry on the Fourth of July.

Anything could happen.

George took a sip of water from the pitcher and spilled some on his chest, watching it dribble and disappear into thickets of hair, chilling the cross on his skin.

American flags hung from windows on both sides of the alley and smaller ones were tied to the branches of rosebushes and stalks of pep-per plants flecked with blossoms.

A gang of boys honked tin horns as they raced bicycles through the alley, the bikes bright with crepe paper—blood red, pearl white, Hellenic blue—noisy with baseball cards clicking against whirling spokes.

George pried his eyes open as the kids ripped past; new Americans born of Old World wombs, little Jimmies flying on tubes of Akron rub-ber and U.S. Steel.

The last boy waved, a dark-haired elf with black eyes, little Georgie just off the boat.

"Mister George," the kid yelled. "Hey Mister George..."

By the time George waved back, he was gone.

George brought the pitcher to his lips, took a sip, and turned it on his face, splashing his eyes and nose and cheeks, rubbing the water into his aching neck when his hand slipped and the pitcher fell.

Slender, banana-shards of glass gleamed like diamonds and George stared at them until they changed colors. When it started to hurt his glance darted down the alley to faded letters on the side of a building.

SHOE REPAIR!

SAVE MONEY!

BE SATISFIED!

"I can't be satisfied," said George, mimicking Muddy on the jukebox.

I am in hell, he thought.

And no one is here but me.

He felt as alone as he did thirty years ago when he got off the boat, a twelve-year-old Greek hillbilly in search of America, the one without limits, the country you were allowed to make up for yourself.

Even then he was determined not to be just another white-aproned Greek cracking eggs over a grill, a house painter, or the baker of bread with coins hidden in the dough.

Three decades later, anyone in East Baltimore could tell you that George Thanos wasn't just another Greek.

A real Greek always knows where his wife is.

The wise men from the Old Country nearly killed themselves getting ahead in America and worked twice as hard to keep their children from succumbing to the culture that made it possible.

After making their last mortgage payment, marrying their strong young Georges to their young virgin Leinis and living long enough to bounce little Jimmies on their knees, the old heads consented to be buried here.

They were protective of George at first and warned him to stay away from cats like Spiro, black people, and women with hair dyed in colors not found in nature.

George passed his hand over the broken glass, close enough to tickle his palm.

The meddlers warned: "Find a good Greek girl before your America swallows you up."

He pushed his hand down hard enough to puncture the skin.

"I found her," he said.

The blues are the facts.

The blues are the truth.

The blues are the roots of everything American.

Shit, thought George, his blood running over the glass. If that's all it takes, I was a citizen the day I stepped off the boat.

Beyond the rooftops, he heard distant sousaphones playing "Stars and Stripes Forever."

Fishing the vodka from his pants, he cracked the seal and swallowed, the clear liquid seeping into his gums, pickling his tongue, firing gummed-up pistons in his head.

Dogs in yards along the alley ran in tight circles and barked the way they did at Orlo's pony every morning.

They yapped at a suitcase gray Mercury, a 1939 sedan packed with guitars, drums, and five men from Chicago by way of the Great Magnolia State.

The Muddy Waters Blues Band had arrived.

Behind the wheel peeped the biggest eyes in the blues, Big-Eye Beetle counting doorways the way he counted out time before every song.

Sitting shotgun, Muddy Waters squinted through the glare on the windshield as the Mercury slowed alongside the Downbeat, his big, Oriental moon of a face turning from side to side as he scolded the drummer for not parking around front where the houses had numbers.

"Safer 'round back boss," said the Beetle. "You know that."

The boss was just thirty-three, young and tough and strong as an ox.

Muddy saw narrow concrete yards divided by thin rows of vegetables, rose bushes and fig trees and he didn't see any black faces except the ones he'd brought.

He saw George Thanos raise himself and stagger to the gate.

"This the Downbeat?" asked the Beetle through the open window, a dozen screen doors in the alley parting to see what new trouble Spiro had imported.

George grabbed the gate post and nodded.

The drummer put the Mercury in park and the band tumbled out, a DJ on the radio predicting heavy humidity and holiday temperatures of ninety-five and above.

George stepped aside to let them pass.

Grabbing black cases rubbed smooth and held together with tape and cracked leather belts, the musicians made their way into the club, arguing about the chances of Eddie Arcaro on Citation back home at Arlington Park.

Spiro rushed outside to greet Muddy, bellowing welcome and letting the musicians know that the Downbeat stood behind all wagers.

Muddy nodded his head toward George and said: "Three to one that cat ain't standin' by showtime."

"Mr. Morganfield," said Spiro, reaching for Muddy's hand. "Mr. Morganfield, this is a great honor. Truly."

"Call me Muddy."

"Muddy," said Spiro. "Come in, please."

Disappearing into the club with his guest of honor, Spiro told George: "Help these gentlemen set up. Bring them whatever they need, some food, a cold drink. Anything."

George lugged in the Beetle's drum kit as the others jostled by, men who smelled of sweat, fried food, and long hours on the road; he tried to make conversation to keep from making trouble.

"Traveling long?"

"A hundred years," said the Beetle.

"Impossible."

"Goddam impossible life."

As he hauled the bass drum in on his back, George's nose caught a sweetness wafting down from Spiro's private office, like a coconut cake left in the oven too long.

He stared up at the open window and pictured the scene: Good booze on the desk, a little sack of seasonings spread across yesterday's paper, and Spiro waiting for the right moment to ask for a song.

Spiro was humored soon enough, music drifting down from the window with smoldering hemp.

"Some nights she don't come home," sang Muddy. "No peoples, sometimes she don't come home at all...the butcher, the baker, the wax dick candlestick maker cry: 'Muddy Water, another mule be kickin' in your stall...'"

George had swallowed a lot of blues in his time and for the past four months the soundtrack to his problems had been Muddy Waters moaning on Spiro's jukebox.

But he'd never heard anything like this.

Creamy as a river bottom, it was not a salve.

Strange and compelling, it brought no comfort.

Deeper than the oceans, it doused nothing.

"All in my sleep, I hear my doorbell ring," sang Muddy, pushing the words around in his mouth before they fell down on George.

"Open the door for my baby, don't see a goddamn thing. I be troubled, all worried in mind. If only I could hold you, could only be satisfied..."

George tapped the Beetle and turned his chin to the window.

"What's he talking about?"

The drummer laughed.

"Somebody usin' what's his and don't belong to nobody else. Tearin' it up, smoothin' it out."

"How do you find out?" asked George.

"You don't know?"

"I know."

"So?"

"To be sure."

"You're not sure."

"Yes."

"You ain't?"

"I'm positive."

"So...?"

"I want to know," said George.

Muddy's wail was harsh, like bleach, and it made George thirsty. He stared at the window and imagined Spiro smiling across the table from the bluesman, as sure as he could see Leini on her back, buried under a shitload of junk.

The drummer looked into George's pathetic face and saw the good burning up with the bad.

"There's a way," he said. "Been a way goin' round in one of the old reels, set down by-and-by..."

"Speak English," said George.

"Ain't everybody knows the half of it."

"But you?" said George, offering his vodka.

"Course I know," said the Beetle, waving off the bottle and reaching into the Mercury for a canvas satchel. "Sure as I'm standing here."

He flipped the keys to the bass player and told everyone to be back a good hour before showtime. George watched the Mercury pull away and knew that Leini could be anywhere.

Smith Island or off in Ethiopia.

"Here," said the Beetle, passing George a sack of silk shirts: sunflower yellow and forest green, maroon guitars hanging on wild vines and Resurrection lilies damp with the sweat from one hundred years of a goddam impossible life.

("I want to be an American, Mr. Spiro...")

("Come around on Sunday mornings and empty the trash for me Georgie, I'll piece you off good, show you the ropes...")

The blues will wash the animosity from your heart.

George would take a life today.

He knew it.

I knew it.

And before Muddy Waters is called back for an encore tonight, you will know it, too.

"My man," said the Beetle, sitting down on the back steps. "Take this laundry upstairs where a colored man can't go. Have me six shirts and two pair of trousers ready by showtime in exchange for one rat trap."

"Yeah?" said George.

"Shit yeah. I gotta get more for it than it cost me. Come tomorrow—if you risk something that matters—its yours to pass on for more than you paid..."

George said he understood.

"Sure you do boss," said the skinny drummer, his palms turned to the rising sun. "But remember, this ain't no pink pillow of Bayer."

"What?"

"No remedy. It's spot remover."

"Okay," said George.

"Okay," said the Beetle. "This is what you gotta do if you wanna make muddy water..."

* * *

The Downbeat faded behind George one sip at a time.

I am being led like a cow, he thought, trudging west in soggy shoes; out of the neighborhood and into the deserted shopping district, toward Orlo's Salvage House down at the end of Clinton Street.

Eastern Avenue was hot and empty, cloaked in a holiday stillness. George didn't even see an open bar.

A few blocks away in Patterson Park, kids raced wheelbarrows and George could hear snare drums and cheers as a hundred immigrants took the oath of citizenship in the annual "I Am An American Day Parade."

Tonight there would be fireworks.

Above his head, the crystal hands of the Great Bolewicki Depression Clock bubbled with water dyed red and blue for the Fourth.

"It's not too late," said the clock. "It's Independence Day all down the line..."

Passing under a black railroad trestle with HIGHLANDTOWN lettered across it, George took a blast from the vodka and moved out of the bridge's shadow and into the sunshine on the other side.

He put his hand over one eye and held the bottle to the sky to see how much was left.

"You're blue man," the Beetle had said. "You been drinkin' from that jug all day, you follow me? That's your blue jug."

At Clinton Street, George turned left and headed for the water, down to a dead-end he'd only been a few times that he could remember.

Once for his wedding reception in a tent behind Ralph's Lunch.

And once again a week later to watch Ralph's burn to the ground.

Each time, George and most everybody but Leini had missed the young junk collector brooding atop the House of Half-Truths across the street; Orlo following Leini's every white-slippered step as she danced on her wedding day; trying to discern what might be saved from Ralph's as the firemen hosed down the rubble.

George measured a pinky's worth of juice left in his pint, shoved the bottle in his pocket and kept moving.

"Fucking witch doctors," he said. "A man would just shoot them both."

A mile-and-a-half away, Spiro begged Muddy Waters to make his guitar sound like a cat being skinned alive.

In a white shingled house on an island near the mouth of the Chesapeake Bay, Orlo fluffed his pillow and asked Leini if she'd ever seen pasta dyed black with squid's ink.

And alone in a corner of the Downbeat, the Beetle nibbled cheese and mustard on white bread and sipped a tall glass of beer; his drum kit assembled on a plywood stage before a mural of a Greek fishing village.

The drummer ate happily, wondering just what it was, precisely, that made it so thrilling to tell stories that weren't true.

People love lies, he decided.

They need them like they need air. Like George Thanos needed alcohol every twenty minutes to keep from seeing things, half of Clinton Street behind him and half yet to go.

The tongue of flame burning atop the Standard Oil refinery burned straight into the nickel haze, no breeze to push it around.

Oil tanks squatted shoulder-to-shoulder on the left, the brown harbor on George's right as a haze rose from asphalt that led the way.

A cat slipped under the claws of a chain-link fence at a trucking company. Clinton Street was filthy with cats in the summer and they froze to death in winter.

George got dizzy from watching them dart from one side of the street to the other.

"A pussy cat," the Beetle had said. "No roosters."

George stumbled forward, eyes peeled for one ready to lose its whiskers. Scheufel's grabbed him first, the only thing besides George open for business as far as the eye could see.

The gin mill was empty except for the owner—a third-generation barmaid named Girlie—and a monkey hanging from water pipes on the ceiling, a chimp in a beanie with "Dinky" embroidered on it.

Dinky'd been hanging at Scheufel's since a sailor on a South American run traded him even-up for a fat bar tab, back when Girlie was a girl.

Other kids had dogs or goldfish, but other kids didn't live on Goose Hill and Girlie taught Dinky to drink beer from a can.

He learned to laugh at the customers on his own.

George took a stool, pointed to the monkey and said: "Gimme what he's having."

Girlie swept the hair back from her face, punctured a pair of triangles in a can of National Boh, and pushed the can across the bar with a small glass. George filled the glass and raised it to Dinky.

"George Thanos," he said. "Glad to meet you."

Dinky screeched and swung down to the other end of the bar as George drained the glass.

(He'd warned Leini the last time, the time before that, and every time he wanted to knock her teeth out: "Don't you ever make a monkey out of me.")

George ordered another beer and shuffled the Beetle's formula in his mind.

Some of it was simple, some was not.

Into George's blue jug had to go the whiskers of a cat, dirt from back doors where the deed was done (the Passover angel didn't have a list so long); something dear traded for something less, and no small part of himself.

"What kind of bullshit is this?" he'd asked.

"The kind you asked for," the drummer replied.

With his third beer, George took a silver dollar from his wallet given to him by Spiro the day he became a citizen.

"Yours," he said, holding the coin in front of Girlie.

"For what?"

"For nothing."

"Nothin's for nothin' Greek."

"A trade."

"For what?"

"For nothing."

Girlie plucked a bobby pin from the thick hive swirling up from her forehead and held it alongside the dollar.

George's free hand took the bobby pin as Girlie grabbed the dollar.

"Okay Girlie," he said, dropping the pin down the neck of the vodka bottle. "Okay for you."

The barmaid drew a fourth beer from the cool box.

"Here," she said. "God bless America."

George shook the vodka in front of a neon light and drained the beer in two gulps.

Outside in the sun, he realized he was drunk again.

"Goddamn," he said. "Goddamn crock of shit."

At Rhode's Shipyard he stopped to watch a billy goat chew weeds in a dusty lot and further down, the Lazaretto Point lighthouse stood dry and chalky alongside the boarded-up Home for Incurables, discarded by the city in a fit of post-war optimism.

At the copper docks, a blue and white tug with ATHENA stenciled on her bow was lashed to an empty barge, reminding George of little boy lessons of gods abandoned in a land where freedom meant making up new mythologies as they were needed.

And where the asphalt stopped, all the way at the end, the red bricks and peaked slate roof of the Goose Hill branch of the Enoch Pratt Free Library stood next to the crumbling foundation that fewer and fewer people remembered as Ralph's Lunch.

Orlo found Leini over a bowl of pig's feet there in the summer of 1926.

They had faithfully repeated the meal once a week ever since; as they did the night before Leini was led to the altar when she told Orlo that she loved him first and the junkman said he understood.

What kind of bullshit?

The kind we ask for.

Across Clinton Street from the outline of Ralph's, the magnificent Salvage House of Leini's beloved loomed before the one she'd never loved, waiting for the derelict steps of George Thanos to violate its secret portals.

George rubbed his eyes at the sight, the harbor sparkling like crinkled brown foil, the sun on the other side of noon and the house of his enemy—SALVAGE across its side in eight-foot high white letters—leaning toward him.

The blue jug dragged George's pants down, exposing the crack of his ass as he wondered why he'd never come down to drag Leini out by her hair.

Why he didn't just burn the place down.

("You don't know?"

"I know."

"So?")

He didn't because he wasn't sure.

A trash barrel overflowed with tuna cans at the seawall and George remembered stories about the cat widows of Clinton Street, women without husbands—some who'd never seen a naked man—lonely do-gooders (our people) who fed stray cats and took the babies home before winter hit.

Leini knew them well enough to say hello to and sometimes gave them a few nickels to buy milk for their darlings.

They blessed her for it, the only blessings that felt right to Leini since she'd begun to lay with Orlo; simple, genuine "God Bless Yous" offered as freely as if she had sneezed.

George shooed flies from the barrel and fished out a can, it's edge orange with rust, wisps of fish stuck in the corners.

Nine cats stuck their heads out from under the crumbling seawall to study him, ducking back when George leaned over to fill the tin with water.

Sitting cross-legged in the street, he dipped his fingers in the can and flicked water on his face; cats in heat leaping across burning rafters in his head and pigeons splitting sunbeams pouring down through holes in the roof of a warehouse on the other side of the street.

"Kitty, kitty," George purred. "Kitty, kitty, kitty."

One walked out from behind a broken cinderblock, the others watching as she stepped close enough to sniff the tin, whiskers like antennae as she bowed to drink, George still as a Buddha.

When the water was gone, the kitten licked flecks of fish from the crevices and George ran his palm along her back, scratching her neck.

"Yata...," he cooed. "Yatoula..."

The kitten stretched and licked the sides of her mouth.

Coaxing the cat into his arms, George cradled her against his shirt, rose to his feet and...

Bang!

Fingers to the kitten's face, a pinch of whiskers yanked from the tender flesh alongside her nose.

The cat squealed and lashed at George, who jerked his head back, but not fast enough, caught just below the left eye, claws digging deep into the drunkard's cheek, dragging down to his chin, the pilfered whiskers sailing off with George's wail.

"AAAAHHHHH!"

Stumbling back, blood streaming down his face, George tightened his left hand around the kitten's neck, sweat and tears stabbing his wounds like needles, screams bouncing off the corrugated walls of the warehouse: "FUCKING PUSSY CAT!"

The Salvage House careened in and out of George's view as he twirled in pain—Leini on her back, Leini on her knees, Leini against the wall—his hands tighter and tighter around the cat's neck as the vodka stripped crusty wax from Girlie's bobby pin.

Vapors of booze bathed the kitten's head as they waltzed, the cat cutting the tip of George's nose with her other paw and biting his upper lip, pinholes leaking blood on yellow teeth.

George growled and hurled the kitten against the metal warehouse.

Neck snapped, she fell dead as George came back to life.

His face burned as he panted in the road and he felt better than he'd had in years.

If it felt this good to kill a cat....

George took his time—a moment to wipe his face and pat the bottle in his pocket, a few more to watch the sun hit the west side of downtown across the harbor—and when he knelt down beside the corpse, its whiskers gave way like strings popping off a fifth grader's violin.

He laughed and his wounds widened, blood dripping cherry from the black stubble on his chin, knowing that the busted onions who charged five bucks to suck the horns off a middle-aged Greek with nothing to live for would charge ten to service the same man with scars on his face.

George pressed the jug to his jaw to bottle his blood together with kitty whiskers that pierced the potion like raw silk from a luminous shawl.

Holding the pint to the sky, he watched his blood mix with ill-will and muddy water: kitty whiskers darting like sperm, Girlie's bobby pin tilting back and forth on its head.

The only ingredients left were back door dirt from the House of Spare Parts.

And a touch of fire.

George picked up the cat by the tail and turned to face the Salvage House, swinging the animal at his side and dragging his feet across Orlo's dry lawn the way Orlo moved his lips between Leini's shoulder blades and Leini could not stop dragging her heart across a field of Stars and Stripes folded neatly into a triangle.

Amidst the clutter of Orlo's acre were crab traps stacked in the shade of a soaring Ailanthus tree on the side of the house; the elements grinding a circle of skeletal jalopies to dust out back.

From the front porch, a wooden pier buckled out into the harbor.

George didn't care how he got inside, he only wanted to hurt something more than he had hurt himself and was too stupid to know it was impossible.

At the back door, he dusted the top step with the edge of his palm, pinching wisps of soot and grime and crumbling them into the neck of the vodka bottle.

The dust drifted down to the venom on the bottom and the pin tinkled against the glass as George shook the bottle to dissolve the dirt.

He tried to peer through the heavy, beveled glass of Orlo's back door and met his reflection instead. He kicked it, succeeding only in rattling the glass.

It was unlocked, a half-turn-of-the-knob between the inside and the outside, left that way in Orlo's haste to drift with Leini in a rowboat floating through the marshes of Smith Isle.

It never occurred to George to try the knob.

Laying the vodka bottle where it would catch the last rays of the sun—the temperature still above ninety with the dinner hour at hand—George pulled the laces from his shoes, braided the strings together and hung the cat from Orlo's back door.

"Salvage this," he said.

It was his last conscious thought before slumping down against the door, the cat swinging gently above his head, drops of blood falling from its mouth and nose into George's hair as I pushed a dream through his black-out, hoping he'd wake up, go home, and do nothing.

But George only stretched in his sleep, shooed the flies buzzing around the open cuts on his face and dreamed of sunlight in an empty room.

Alone on the floor sat a woman years removed from Leini's womb and the night Muddy Waters came to Baltimore to sing the blues.

She looked like Leini.

Just like Leini.

Except that her eyes were too close together.

Or were they too far apart?

A beauty fouled by the vengeance of a lunatic; fathered by insanity or love but not by both, the Retarded Princess of Clinton Street sitting half-a-bubble off plumb in an Abdicated Castle of Junk bequeathed to her when the last of her parents was dead.

Her unborn life dependent upon the choices George would make in the next ten minutes.

It was dark when the back door fell open, waking George as he tumbled in from a nap long enough for his potion to cook and cool in the sun, a hot breeze wafting over the fresh, yolky scabs on his face.

(I opened the door to save Orlo the trouble of repairing it later.)

George was hungover again.

How many matches can you put to a spent wick?

Back at the Downbeat, the biggest eyes in the blues banged out time on a cow bell; the drummer's thin back covered in fresh linen as he laid down the beat behind a book of sad stories tumbling from the jowls of Muddy Waters.

"I be troubled, all troubled in mind," Muddy howled as Idiot George retrieved his bottle from the yard. "Cain't tell lies from the truth, just cain't be satisfied..."

Stumbling inside, George waved his pint around like a man shaking off advice that only makes him mad; all of the cool, dark air inside Orlo's sucked out into the night as every conflicted spirit who'd found sanctuary there got the hell out of George's way.

George steadied himself on the kitchen table, feeling his way in the dark as his eyes adjusted, a milky glow on the varnished table top from harbor lights and stars drifting through the open back door.

George recognized Orlo's Fedora hanging on a nail and on his second pass around the table spied a bottle of cooking wine.

He put the junkman's hat on his head and grabbed the bottle, tossing the cork into a front room where it disappeared in clutter as he turned the bottle upside down in his mouth.

Resuming his walk, he was stopped by the gleaming enamel of a new refrigerator and stared hard at it.

Even Spiro didn't have an electric ice-box at home. George finished the wine, threw the bottle into the front room and grabbed a chair to sit before the fridge.

A big, upright slab of humming white metal with rounded edges and a wide, smooth door, it was the only thing Orlo had ever bought new for himself, an everyday luxury of modern America that kept meat fresh for days.

Caught in the machine's translucent gleam, George licked his lips and admired the perfect fit of his cuckold's chapeau before jerking his head violently to free himself of it.

As it hit the floor, he kicked it into the front room with the rest of the junk, the face in the fridge was traumatized enough to be his own.

"No one will tell you, but I will. I have watched them for years...filthy pork...week after week...like no one has ever prepared it before. No accidents on Clinton Street."

Aghast, George let his elbow slip off the table, cracking his funny bone. Pain shot up through his jaw as he knocked over the vodka bottle, a small crack in its neck deep enough for the potion to leak across the table, a running puddle that stopped at the edge as a Greek chorus chanted: "Muddy water, muddy water...another spoon be slidin' in yo' drawer..."

When George opened the refrigerator, light rushed into the room; the box clean and empty except for a carafe of ice water capped with a whittled cork.

A cold mist poured out with the light, washing over the crusted wounds on George's face, electric light skimming energy from the puddle on the table, cold stinging George's nostrils, frosting the tips of his ears.

He opened the freezer box, its walls bearded with frost and found bundles packaged in white butcher's paper, dated in Leini's handwriting for this week, next week, and the week after that, an edible calendar of assignations.

Fondling them like a blind man running his fingers over a stranger's face to guess their ancestry, George discovered that they weren't flat, like steaks or chops, and they weren't curved, like ribs.

Severed flush at one end; bumpy and almost square at the other, the meat was blunt, like a cudgel.

George grabbed the package marked for the coming week—Leini, it seemed, was coming back—and kicked the door closed.

He laid it on a part of the table that wasn't wet and carefully unwrapped the paper, smoothing it out with his fingertips.

In the center lay sticks of gray meat and gristle.

"I feel like snappin' a razor in her face," Muddy sang up the road. "Let some boneyard be her restin' place..."

Another fine evening at the Downbeat.

Everyone had a good time and no excuses were made for George.

George pulled the paper out from under the trotters like a magician yanking a cloth from a table set for two, and with the edge of his fingernails he rolled the knuckles into the radiant ichor.

If the witch drowns, she is innocent.

Extracting Girlie's bobby pin from the cracked neck of the bottle, George ran it across his teeth and tightened his lips around it before using his tongue to push it out like a cherry stem.

He used the pin to tenderize the pork—stabbing it, over and over—and rubbed his poison into the holes; adulterating the delicacy with an invisible lovers' litmus, guaranteeing for the rest of his miserable life not that he would be free or healed or loved, but that every time anyone met him in the company of the child soon to be born to Leini they would walk away wondering just what, precisely, was so wrong with the girl.

Orlo and Leini Take the Train

PIN-RAYS OF SUNLIGHT BEAR DOWN through black glass and dance in the dark circles under Leini's eyes, tiny beams of color crossing a face creased with despair.

Leini tilts her head back on a mahogany bench in the marble train station, the grand Acropolis of the Pennsylvania Line at Charles and Mount Royal in Baltimore.

She tries to rest—to be rested enough to recognize help if it appears—but she cannot.

Leini opens her eyes and stares at the dome of stained glass in the railway roof, all twenty-three diametrical feet of its cathedral brilliance dead and mute under thick black paint; dead like Leini except for thin rays of high noon pushing down through chips in the skylight's ebony coat.

Rainbow glass tarred a dozen years ago to give the Axis one less target.

"Almost ten years the war's over, ten years my Jimmy's gone," thinks Leini, wondering if the black glass is an agitation or a comfort to her. "Ten years, still black."

The junkman of Clinton Street sits four rows behind his lover, watching splinters of light move yellow and red across a face he has kissed for nearly thirty years; green and blue tracing a face that hasn't smiled in ten.

Orlo and Leini wait for the 2:12 Oriole Wing to New York City.

Off to see a specialist named Yang.

Orlo found the doctor in crumbling newsprint folded inside a book of nursery rhymes tossed out with the trash behind Binney Street.

"HERB DOCTOR OF CHINATOWN DELIVERS MIRACLE CURES."

From his Salvage House, Orlo crossed the street to the Goose Hill branch of the Enoch Pratt Free Library and, although the newspaper clipping was more than twenty years old, found Yang in a Manhattan phone directory.

The next morning, a letter sailed from the foot of Clinton Street to Yang's sprawling apartment on Mott Street.

"She's stuck," the junkman wrote. "We're stuck."

A week later, an answer arrived in small script: "Yang will try."

Orlo walked Leini to the end of the pier that juts out from his front yard toward Fort McHenry and made his pitch.

"Okay," said Leini. "Give me a week to come up with something to tell George."

As if George could tell lies from linseed oil.

And three days later, on a humid Saturday morning in July of 1955, Leini left her husband at the kitchen table with a bottle of vodka and his hair in knots; Orlo locked the Salvage House behind him and uptown on Charles Street the Oriole Wing waited for all to board.

* * *

They met a few years before Depression hit, over a bowl of pig's feet in a working man's lunch room down at the end of Clinton Street.

Leini was seventeen, virgin, and Greek.

Orlo would never be any of those things.

From that day, they nurtured a love forbidden first by her family and then, after Leini bowed her head to marry a man chosen for her, by the God of the Greek Orthodox Church.

I knew you first she would tell Orlo on his bad days, no need to say that she loved him first because there never was anyone else.

You are the one I chose.

That first day, in cattycorner booths nearest the kitchen at Ralph's Lunch, over wooden bowls of pig's feet simmered in a thin broth of tomato and basil, Leini severed her heart from her family's bridle and allied it to the care of a blue-eyed American who roamed the alleys of Baltimore in search of treasure.

Thisavros.

The only word of Greek Orlo took the trouble to learn on his own, apart from what he picked up from the torrents Leini summoned when she was excited, afraid, or angry.

Evrika to thisavro vois mou.

The way other people called their lover sweetheart.

They were sweethearts from the early evening in the Summer of 1926 when Leini first ladled out sweet digits of swine for Orlo, stealing away as often as possible to share the delicacy and one another.

It grew to ritual: one week Orlo cooked, the next week Leini, back and forth; a delicious game of catch stretching through the years, always something new—the excitement of finding something—and a story to go with it.

When it is your turn to cook, labor to outdo the last meal.

If you are the guest, be attentive and do as you're told.

It was fun in the beginning, the Salvage House their Hollywood wardrobe for dress-ups. They came at odd hours from different directions to meet in secret for an hour or two, ferrying kettles of pig's feet into the woods behind the bottlecap factory; making campfires in the sooty marshes of Sparrows Point, a small pot on burning sticks as the Bethlehem Steel plant vibrated in the distance, the aroma of slow-cooked pork mixing with the stench of molten steel.

"Look!" Orlo would cry, pointing across the Patapsco to the tin mill. "The Parthenon!"

They rendezvoused in a suite of rooms at the top of the Bromo Seltzer Tower, the office of a big-shot who traded Orlo the use of a small kitchen and big sofa for the pick of that week's alley harvest.

And they received prudent messengers bearing maps leading to the scent of fresh pork.

Which so many yesterdays ago meant Smith Island, today means a marble train station, and the day after tomorrow will seem no more exotic than a dog chasing its tail.

* * *

Getting up to stretch his legs, Orlo looks at Leini across the length of Penn Station and remembers the last time she cooked with any zeal, back before Jimmy was killed, the last time she wanted to play.

She'd told him to dress like a chef and bring canvas pastry tubes of icing, heavy tubes with thick nozzles he had to buy at a bakery supply. She told him to leave the pony home and meet her just past dawn in an orange brick rowhouse a few blocks from her own in the 600 block of South Macon Street.

Orlo climbed the white marble steps and heard Gerswhin through the open slats of a jalousie door.

Leini snatched the chef's hat from Orlo's head at the door, took his hand and said: "Bring the icing."

Climbing the stairs behind her, he glimpsed a table in the parlor set with Limoges, linen, and silver; a table set for lunch although light had barely cracked the day, the house cool and empty except for Orlo and Leini and a cauldron of pig's feet simmering in a broth of pearl onions and peppercorns.

In the front bedroom, they took turns reading to each other and made love in a bed beneath a statue of Saint Lucy with her eyes set before her on a platter.

On either side of Lucy: photographs of someone else's family—stern husband, a wife without expression, and three smiling children looking down on Orlo and Leini as sunlight moved through venetian blinds to cast stripes of shadow and light across their skin.

Such fun.

* * *

Leini wears her habit today, her best disguise ever; the one that makes her invisible, that she will not surrender: mourning dress from shawl to shoes, just another aging Greek woman in black with swollen ankles and a bad heart.

Orlo circles the station, moving closer. He watches Leini take a novel out of her bag and from it remove an envelope that has marked her place in every book she has read for eleven years.

From the envelope she gently pulls a letter that has survived a thousand unfoldings. On wisps of pulp, it endures another.

Orlo reads his lover's lips as his lover reads the letter, mouthing its contents in unison with her like a bored priest at morning Mass.

"Dear Ma, it's almost over and I'm almost home...I found a swell recipe for pig's feet in an old bookstore over here, maybe one you don't know. A nice girl here translated it for me (she's real cute, Ma, wait'll you meet her, I know you won't mind that she's not Greek).

"It calls for vinegar and nutmeg and you serve it with sweet red cabbage and roasted apples. Enjoy it with your friend and think of me when you make it. You can be happy now, Mama. It's almost over. I'm coming home."

Leini rubs the envelope against her cheek.

"Love, Jimmy," she whispers.

Orlo blows air through his mouth, tips his hat back on his head and ambles toward his bench, remembering what Leini had said the day Jimmy's letter arrived.

From the black wall phone in her kitchen, liberated by what she had feared since the day her son was born, she said: "Orlo, he knows. He knows and it's okay. Red cabbage and apples! Orlo! Maybe it's time. Maybe when Jimmy comes home we can change this thing around."

Later that same day, the phone at the Salvage House rang again.

"Orlo, he's dead," she cried with the telegram in her hands. "My Jimmy's dead. He knew and he's dead."

Leini took the news as the consequence of choices she could not change, changing Orlo forever as his lover went down with her grief.

* * *

"ALL ABOARD THE PENNSY LINE, 2:12 ORIOLE WING TO WILMINGTON, 30TH STREET PHILADELPHIA, NEWARK, AND THE LAND OF MANHATTOES BELTED ROUND BY WHARVES...."

* * *

Leini boards the train five cars up from Orlo and takes a seat in a chair car, a floating living room of worn furniture and carpet from the days when there were more red-blooded keisters in trains than cars.

She stares out the window as they pull out and wonders what a nut doctor named Yang can possibly tell her that she doesn't already know; the train moving with a slow click and roll as a black sky-light, the City of Baltimore and another hot afternoon in July fade behind her.

Orlo sits in a smoking car an eighth-of-a-mile behind Leini, not quite ready to light the cigar in his hands, watching as the station platform gives way to freight yards full of old black men and the blur of downtown as the Oriole Wing gathers speed.

All this trouble, he thinks, nothing but trouble and even now, on a fast train out of town, she will not let me sit beside her in public.

I am fifty-eight years old, an old man getting older without children or grandchildren to help me pull this pathetic wagon of lies.

Keep going, no matter what happens. Once we hit Manhattan, let's just keep going.

He wonders if they'll get the chance to share a bowl of pig's feet in New York and his mouth waters, a picture in his mind of Leini sleeping in a bed of their own.

Stupid game. He wants to race up the aisle and scream in her face: You never sprinkle the nutmeg or bake the apples.

That was in the letter.

You and your friend enjoy.

That was in there too.

On her best days, the most Leini can manage is a boiled potato on the side; this from a woman who once boned and marinated six pig's feet for a week before stuffing them with spinach, minced truffles, Italian bread crumbs, garlic and mushroom, all under her husband's nose.

Now, in the mixed-up world of color television and polio vaccines, rocket ships and rock-and-roll, Orlo and Leini sit in separate cars on a northbound train to see a Chinaman who heals with dried roots and a sharp tongue.

Orlo lights his cigar and waits for the match to burn his thumb.

"A goddamn witch doctor," he says.

* * *

Ribbons of purple silk studded with gems.

Strings of seashells.

And the carved bones of small animals.

A curtain that parts upon the brow of a young boy.

"Dr. Yang will see you now."

Orlo helps Leini up and they step across the sparkling threshold and into Yang's examining room, an octagon split by narrow hallways shooting off to God knows where.

"Mr. Junkman," says Yang, shaking Orlo's hand.

"This is Leini," says Orlo and the doctor steps forward and bows.

Yang looks back and forth between the two and finds sad and sadder, no way and maybe, too late and just in time. He knows he cannot help them both—certainly not at the same time—but that is not what people come to hear.

"Why need Yang?"

Orlo has an urge to speak, to do for Leini what she has not been able to do for herself.

The junkman hesitates, knowing they'll never get what he wants if he lets her tell it.

Leini opens her mouth and more words than she has spoken in five months spill out.

"Doctor, it hurts...locked up the whole time I was growing up, everywhere I went somebody watching and waiting to tell someone else where they saw me and what I'd been doing...I could never make myself small enough. Orlo showed me how to be invisible and we went anywhere we wanted and it was so much fun to move through the world like that that I wanted it all the time. It was good for a long time and then they killed my Jimmy and I was back in the old place after all those years and I can't find the way out..."

Leini's eyes are dry, she bites her lip and twirls her wedding ring on her pinky, forcing it over her thumb, over fat, dry knuckles until she bleeds.

"Jimmy will be thirty this year," she says. "He never comes home."

Yang paces, a finger to his lips.

"Mr. Junkman," he commands. "Go down to street. At end of block turn right. Down to middle of next block is alley, turn left. Alley take you to butcher shop on sidewalk. Can't miss: carcass hang from bamboo poles—pig, goose, and lamb. There find Tim, butcher. From Tim buy feet of one sow, not too old. Tell Tim—want sow more young than old. Four feet. Boy will wait for you."

Orlo looks at Leini and then at Yang.

"Go," the doctor says.

Halfway through the purple curtain, Orlo turns his back and asks a question that has simmered in his gut with cartilage and cabbage for thirty years, one that nearly knocks Leini off the low stool where she waits for Yang to lay a stethoscope to the pulse in her neck.

Feebly, the junkman asks: "What do I get out of it?"

"DINNER!" roars Yang and Orlo shoves off like a man who's been beaten across the shoulders.

Alone with Leini, the doctor moves along the periphery of the room, ranging between high shelves and glass cabinets, pinching stems and blossoms and piling them together with petals and roots on a chopping block in the middle of the room.

Yang gathers orange blossoms, a giant rafflesia and dogtooth violets and over them shreds a young Ailanthus tree—no more than a weed, really—before working the pile over with a sharp knife.

"Talk," he says.

Leini slips a hand inside of her blouse and stares at her shoes.

"I told you, it hurts. Sometimes the pain wakes me up. Like my heart is pulling away from itself. I don't think it's in my head."

"Everything in head," says Yang, using his blade to scrape the chopped flowers back to the middle of the block before going over them again. "Maybe coming, maybe going, but always in head.

"Lie is like cannibal," he says. "Never satisfied."

"I just hold on," says Leini.

"Hold on scared," says Yang, sprinkling drops from a blue bottle over the pile, chopping it into a moist powder.

"It's my only happiness," Leini argues.

Yang puts his face near the chopping block and blows softly, drying the herbs with his breath.

"That is why you come to see Yang? Because you are happy?"

The question stabs Leini. She wants to cry.

"Help me," she says.

"Help self," says Yang, pinching the powder into small linen pouches and tying them with string cooks use to truss fowl.

"I just hold on."

"Maybe should let go."

Seven blocks away, as Orlo dumbly watches a hag named Tim hack at the shins of a dead female pig, the Junkman of Clinton Street feels his intestines fall down to his scrotum.

Yang stands before Leini with three pouches of herbs in his palm: No. 1, No. 2, and No. 3.

"Must move to start," he says and when Leini finally takes the herbs from him, he shows her the door and calls his next patient.

Orlo returns with bundles in white butcher's paper, met outside of Yang's office by Leini and the house boy. The junkman tries to give the packages to the boy and the kid pushes them away, leading the lovers down a hallway to a small kitchen.

Stopping at the door, the boy points to the pig's feet, the herbs in Leini's hand, and the stove.

"Her turn, yes?"

"It is," says Leini and the boy disappears.

On top of a porcelain enamel gas range sits a large aluminum pot. A pink Formica table set for two hugs a wall divided by a porthole that looks over the meat packing district.

Leini takes the pork from Orlo and unwraps it in the sink, the counter laid out with prepared goodies: sliced ginger, ingots of brown sugar, a bottle of black vinegar, and three brown eggs.

Orlo roots through bins for the cursed head of cabbage.

"Did you tell Yang it was your turn?"

"No," says Leini, bringing each of the pouches to her nose and her lips.

Tacked into stained plaster behind the stove is a thin strip of rice paper marked in Yang's tiny script and splattered with grease.

"Boil...drain...rinse...scrape...rinse..."

It says: "Use all herbs. Eat to finish."

Leini follows Yang's recipe to the pinch and drop.

Orlo struggles with small talk, trying to believe that one meal is going to make any difference, forgetting that the first one did, ignorant that any difference is all the difference.

He comes up behind Leini and puts his arms around her waist as she lowers the eggs into boiling water.

Orlo tickles her, trying to add a dollop of laughter to the recipe, teasing: "You believe any of this?"

"You're going to make me break the eggs," she scolds, prying his hands away to sprinkle the first pouch into the water, watching the herbs churn with the eggs.

On a back burner, the vinegar bubbles in a shallow pan. In it, Leini dissolves the brown sugar and a second pouch of herbs.

Confidence rushes through Orlo as he watches Leini cook. He kisses her neck and says: "We can do anything we want."

"Let's just get through the meal."

When the pig's feet have finished cooking, Leini takes them from the pot, drains them on the sideboard and cuts the meat from the bone, laying chunks of pork in an oval dish and setting it on the table.

She cracks the soft-boiled eggs and scoops the goo over the pork, pouring the vinegar and brown sugar sauce into a gravy boat in the shape of a junk.

Over everything—across the universe—she sprinkles the contents of the last pouch, tosses her apron on the sink and says, sitting down, "It's ready."

They eat for nearly an hour, slow and steady without saying much, waiting for the roof to open up and God to come down, break bread and fly them up to heaven.

The dinner is exquisite.

Sweet and vague and sour and familiar.

Like none before, as always.

Yet the lovers dine with effort, swallowing the meat like a sick kid trying to choke down a horse pill.

The meal began with nine hunks of pork between them and when they have each eaten four, Orlo clears his mouth with water, spears the last piece, and pops it in his mouth.

Leini looks at him as if he has grabbed the last life preserver on a sinking ship.

Shredding the meat with his teeth, Orlo gets up from his chair and moves around the table to Leini, swallowing half of the meat and holding the rest in his cheek, pig fat and herbs seeping into his jaw through the cracks in his gums.

Too full to move, Leini looks up as Orlo begins to rewrite Yang's precise instructions.

Straddling Leini, the junkman pins her in the chair and grips her wrists above her head.

Parting her lips with his own, he transfers the last of the meat to her mouth, pushing it to the back of her throat with his tongue, shoving until she swallows her share of the last odd piece.

Orlo licks the sticky sauce from Leini's lips, his saliva mixing with the food and herbs in her mouth.

"Water," she says.

Orlo brings a glass to her mouth and Leini gulps it down. When he tries to set it back on the table it teeters and falls, rolling to the edge without dropping off.

Orlo licks drops of water from the corners of Leini's mouth and with every bit of strength left to him at fifty-eight—old and getting older, no children or grandchildren to comfort him—lifts her black dress, yanks her cotton panties down to shoes only a nun should wear, and takes her in the kitchen chair.

With each scrape of the chair against the linoleum, Yang's herbs seep further into their blood and as Orlo savors the best sex he has had in eleven years, he wonders if the magic in his veins will reach his semen by the time his semen reaches Leini.

Orlo spins like a wheel and shoots a blinding constellation across a long arc, wondering if a forty-six-year-old woman might conceive a tableside miracle in Chinatown.

"Don't stop," moans Leini, lifting a leg to the table. "Not yet."

Orlo mixes it up a little longer until his beloved joins him on the other side and they cling to one another.

"Man," says Orlo.

"Jesus," says Leini.

In gasps and whispers, they say how much they love each other.

Up or down.

Pig's feet or porridge.

Holy Land or hell.

Pulling back, they look for clues in each other's eyes but see only their own reflections.

Orlo lays his forehead against Leini's.

"You don't look any different."

"Neither do you."

He climbs off of her and moves to the sink, cupping water in his hands and splashing his face. Leini uses a napkin next to her plate to wipe the trickle on her thighs, tosses it on the table and heaves up her drawers.

Orlo follows her out of the room, snatching the recipe from the tack on the wall and shoving it in his pocket.

They ask to see Yang before they leave, but are refused.

"Yang done," says the house boy, handing Orlo a bill for eleven dollars and a promise to always give in to Leini's wishes.

Orlo gives the boy a ten and a one and tips the kid a buck while Leini inspects the baubles on the purple ribbon separating her from the examining room, wondering if they are real.

Brushing close to the curtain, she hears a woman tell Yang how much it hurts.

But she cannot make out the doctor's response.

* * *

The Oriole Wing glides south to Penn Station; the marble hall quiet and empty, black night filling chips in paint used to silence a rainbow.

The tarred rooftops of East Baltimore zip by like black hats sewn together at their brims, each one adorned with a small brick chimney in the shape of an A.

One after the other, rowhouse after rowhouse of families sleep with their secrets as the Holy Land passes in the moonlight.

Orlo stares at the passing city, a rolling wave of white marble and orange brick.

People who can't sleep sit on the sidewalk in folding chairs, catching a breeze in the middle of the night, sipping something cold and making conversation as Orlo sits next to Leini in a deserted rail car.

In one of these houses is Leini's husband, their seven-year-old daughter and framed pictures of Jimmy alongside the bed where Leini will sleep tonight.

Orlo fingers Yang's bill in his pocket and wonders how he could possibly surrender anymore to anyone than he has from the moment he met the round-faced beauty with a mouth like a baby's heart.

All those years ago in a Greek lunch room called Ralph's down at the end of Clinton Street.

Long enough to find a small fortune among the debris of other people's lives, to bury two horses, stuff a third, and wear out a heavy truck; time enough to build a Salvage House library with more recipes for the meat above the hooves of swine than will ever be amassed in France.

Tonight he has another, a story to go with it, and the traces of magic herbs beneath the nails of every finger on his right hand.

Orlo turns from the window as the light of the station beckons beyond the bend.

"I love you little girl," he says.

Leini wakes from a shallow nap and closes the book in her lap. She kisses the junkman on the cheek and gives him a gentle push on the arm as the train begins to slow.

"Better scoot back," she says. "We're home."

The
Annunciation

IN THE BRIEF MOMENT before the Great Bolewicki Depression Clock swept past the end of the millennium, the restless spirit of Elvis Presley returned to Earth through the newly ripened womb of a fifteen-year-old Jewish virgin named Ruthie as the girl floated helplessly over the rooftops of Baltimore.

The clock said: "It's not too late, it's only..."

And a new age of revolution began ticking away.

The good news was heralded throughout the Cosmos, but passed unnoticed on the blue planet where it was rendered; a fantastic event absent from Ruthie's agenda.

"Ready?" the angel asked.

"Am I ready?" shrieked Ruthie.

"Ready or not..." said the angel.

"Oh no," moaned Ruthie, breaking down.

"Oh yes," said the angel.

"Oh God," cried Ruthie.

"That's right."

* * *

Ruth Hadassah Singer had the face of a cherub, eyes like golden pools, an arrogant mind, and an obstinate heart.

By the tenth grade, she was certain that any success and all reward was hers for the choosing.

All so pretty and plausible.

So sure and sweet.

All before the choosers chose Ruthie.

The girl spent most of her time reading about the gardens of Monet, practicing the violin, hanging out at lacrosse games, talking on a private line in her private room, and shopping with inexhaustible plastic.

It was the life she was born for.

But when privilege dimmed to predictability and entitlement bought nothing not expected, Ruthie liked to go slumming in the Holy Land.

Always with an accomplice along for the ride, she would cut school early and drive down to the waterfront and a corner gin mill consecrated in pink and black as a shrine to the King of Rock-and-Roll.

Down to Miss Bonnie's Elvis Grotto: Graceland on the Patapsco.

Where she felt invisible and safe in the long shadow of the King.

Protected by the blessings of Miss Bonnie, Ruthie drank on the sly and drove middle-aged men crazy in her white blouses and pleated skirts, wading just close enough to the undertow to feel its pull.

When the stupid men and their stupid tricks bored her, Ruthie would ask Miss Bonnie for stories about the days when men pushed handcarts and grinding stones up and down the alleys; strong men who sold pots and pans and sharpened knives, men like Ruthie's great-grandfather, who came to America with nothing.

"Aww, I was a little girl back then, hon," the barmaid would tell her. "Hell, I was younger than you are now."

Through all her years of serving up eight-ounce draughts, boiled eggs, pickled pig's feet and as much Elvis Presley as Baltimore could handle—her feet swelled from standing all day, ears rattling with the nonsense of drunks and her eyes burning with smoke—Miss Bonnie's comfort came first and always from the King.

Soothed by the luxury of his voice and the multiplication of his image, she would take a moment from her labors to glance around the sanctuary and say: "No matter which way I turn, he's always smiling at me."

And now, twenty-two years after Presley's death, Bonnie's homage had paid off.

A wide stream of people looking for something and willing to trade dollars on the chance that it existed in the voice of the King had made Miss Bonnie a wealthy woman, with the hard-earned right to sit deep in an easy chair, smoking cigarettes, sipping wine, receiving visitors, and watching her boy sing to her and only her on a television as wide as the wall.

Now Elvis was just another cartoon to Ruthie and when she thought Miss Bonnie was distracted she would ridicule the rich failure of his life.

"You'd think if you were born that lucky you'd be smart enough to hold onto it."

Bonnie ignored Ruthie's bad manners in favor of something shining in the girl's eyes, a glint that gave her hope against the bad roads she saw there.

When the wine was going down easy, the barmaid would preach from her chair, bragging on her little high school friends, girls with more education in their toes than all of her regulars put together, kids who came to visit more than her own grandchildren.

At the first sight of Ruthie and her girlfriends slipping in the side door, Miss Bonnie would crow: "Here come my darlin's. All the way from up'air in Rollin' Park. Aww yeah, up'air where the shit don't stink."

Up there where neither shit nor sin stank.

Up in the rarefied air where Ruthie drove her Daddy's Jaguar to buy hamburgers and learned black history from the personal life of her housekeeper; a child for whom sneaking down to the corner of Fleet and Port streets to drink and tell lies was more exciting than shuttling to the moon, which, for Ruthie, was also an option.

Sweet Virgin Ruthie.

The young and arrogant.

Ruthie who snuck down to the Grotto as often as she could, to be present in a place where things happened that no one could stop from happening.

Like Miss Bonnie's faith and fortune, upon which the barmaid commissioned a hot-air balloon shaped to the last curve and crevice like the magnificent head of Elvis Presley; a $120,000 marvel tethered fast to the roof, the King's eyes piercing the night like blue lights, just hours away from its maiden voyage.

The balloon was Miss Bonnie's thank-you and she passed over all of the youngsters in her own family to offer the first ride to Ruthie.

She said: "You know darlin', I believe in God and my certain saints...hell, you just don't turn your back on those who helped you up."

Up, up, and away.

The King had delivered.

And would soon be delivered again.

The night before her ride, Ruthie was sitting in the back of the Grotto with a classmate, drinking beer, listening to the King sing of wise men and lonely streets, and flirting with a couple of guys twice her age; stringing the simpletons along for the kick of seeing their eyes pop and their lips twitch when she crossed her legs or licked bubbles from the corners of her mouth.

Ruthie's friend was named Carla, sixteen with orange hair and freckles, a sexual veteran out of fear, refusing to be bound by anything she didn't know.

Ruthie was a year younger, with nut brown hair and ocher eyes, a virgin because of what she didn't want to know and intending to keep it that way.

The man who craved Ruthie had a vague idea that his desire could only turn out wrong and he had some shame for even trying; but he'd never seen a peach quite so ripe and precious as the girl sitting next to him and he was willing—in the part of his brain that showed movies on a very small screen—to strangle a yard full of dogs just to dip his cookie in Ruthie's warm bowl of milk.

His lust for her was so great it projected itself on the wall behind the child's head in twisted neon.

"Whatever makes you happy," he told her. "Whatever you want to do..."

And Ruthie pushed her empty glass toward him again.

From her stuffed chair in the back, with one eye on Elvis and the other on her livelihood, Miss Bonnie regulated the game, ready to give the men their walking papers if they got too far out of line.

"At dawn," said Carla, and Ruthie kicked her under the table.

"What?" said the men.

"The balloon leaves at dawn," she said, and Ruthie kicked her again.

"We'll come see you off," said the man who wanted Carla.

"Yeah," said Ruthie's hopeless suitor. "We'll come and kiss you bon-voy-ah-gee."

Ruthie smiled into the man's delusion and purred: "Right, asshole. And I'm Cleopatra."

* * *

A dozen balloons lay limp and flat on the rolling lawn around the Patterson Park Pagoda, a strange and skeletal obelisk of the Orient a block away from Bonnie's bar, a three-tiered jewel stuck in the bleeding heart of the Holy Land.

Balloons majestic and ridiculous—vast swaths of nylon shaped like spark plugs and eggplants and sea lions greeted Ruthie and a hangover that nagged: "You shouldn't have...but you did...and now you're here..."

Stepping carefully through the early morning darkness, Ruthie made her way through a maze of wicker gondolas and the people attending to them, her tired eyes straining for Elvis through the shadows as day broke around the narrow rows of houses flanking the Great Bolewicki Depression Clock.

The clock's crystal hands were filled with bubbling water and its face glowed through the promise of dawn.

"It's not too late," it said. "It's only a quarter to six in the morning."

Ruthie didn't see Carla anywhere.

Typical, she thought, perturbed but not unnerved, drawn to the thrill waiting for her and eager to add it to her collection.

Ruthie walked by a group of people working to inflate an antique balloon, a bulb of a single color shaped like nothing except for what it was. Behind it, she found Elvis, his sideburns laying on the grass like a couple of giant, burnt pork chops.

Next to the balloon stood a man to whom Ruthie would entrust her life hundreds of feet above the ground.

Gus was in his forties but he looked a hard sixty, with a flask on his hip and a throbbing strawberry on his nose, a sky pilot who had seen many a morning but none more perfect for sailing than this.

Gus was fiddling with a gas generator and a big industrial fan when Ruthie asked, without introduction, if he had seen a red-haired girl named Carla.

Gus yanked a cord on the generator and with a whir and a whoosh the fan spun with the might of a hundred horses, filling out the folds and creases in the giant envelope flapping on the ground.

The balloon grew before the girl like a giant mushroom—eighty feet tall with a pompadour on top—and by the time Ruthie scratched her pretty head and blinked twice, its regal visage was upright and proud amidst a field of eleven competitors made from the same material, filled with the same energy, but dwarfed in the mighty shadow of the King.

"Damn," said one man. "Wouldja look'it that."

It was a simple race. One balloon sailed away first and the rest took off after it.

Today, they would all chase Elvis.

Ruthie looked around the hillside as the park began to fill and she knew that Carla was not going to show.

"Get in," the pilot barked.

Ruthie dawdled to defy the man, finishing her coffee and letting the cup fall to the ground, inching just close enough to the gondola for Gus to hear her complaints about unworthy friends, the stupidity of a balloon shaped like Elvis Presley and the empty lives of the people who gathered in awe around his billowing head.

Putting brown, wrinkled face an inch from the young beauty, the pilot said: "Missie, if you're lucky, the world will beat that shit out of you. If you ain't, you're gonna be ruled by it for the rest of your life."

"Uh-huh," said Ruthie, moving toward the gondola on baby steps, just frightened enough to ask an honest question.

"Are you sure it's a good day for this?"

Gus scanned the sky and found it as clear as Ruthie's complexion.

"Aww yeah Missie," he said. "There's a storm comin' and we're gonna ride it."

Ruth decided that the man was an idiot and her courage returned.

Laying the soft curve of her ass on the railing of the small basket, she swung her feet over the side as the crowd pushed in closer, noisy and excited as the countdown began and a happy double-pump of accordions and clarinets rained down from a polka band on the third tier of the Pagoda.

The band played the "In the Clouds Polka," the crowd cheered, and the sun broke free from the last gray cloud of dawn as Gus followed Ruthie into the gondola, handing her a sack of rocks to toss over the side on the count of three.

Ruth cradled the weight in her arms, the balloon chafed at its tether, and when the pilot unleashed a jet of raw heat that pushed the battle between bondage and flight to its limit, the girl thought she saw something gold sparkling inside the flame.

"One...," called Gus, "two...three..."

Ruthie counted to four and dropped the sack.

The balloon shot up like a rocket!

With each roaring gust of flame it sailed higher in the sky, slowing from a streak to a gentle waft as the distance grew between Elvis and the Earth.

Ruthie loved it.

Before the faces on the ground faded to specks, she saw the man who had bought her drinks at the Grotto the night before, a man who would have cut off his limbs to feel his lips on hers but was not yet availed of that opportunity as he ran on crazy legs and waved eager arms in pursuit of the spot where Ruthie had been just a moment before.

Tilting back his neck until his head touched his shoulders, the man blew kisses and shouted words of affection that died before finding their mark.

Ruthie leaned over the side and laughed long and hard, her hangover melting in her glee, the pain of it dripping down upon the man's face like yolk.

With Elvis weaving through the clouds, the other balloons were cut loose for the chase and a happy Ruthie Singer sailed away from her troubles.

She strained to make out the ruby gleam of her Daddy's car and then relaxed to cast a wider gaze across East Baltimore: the eight-sided slate roof of the Pagoda, brick chimneys on black-tarred rowhouse roofs, and a field of tombstones like Popsicle sticks in the O'Donnell Street boneyard where a crew of Chinese sailors were buried after the Baltimore hailstorm of 1917.

Tracing the harbor rim, Ruthie looked down on the twin gold cupolas of Saint Casimir's Roman Catholic Church, where old Polish ladies with hard faces and thick ankles prayed to Buczha, retired packing house women with the ancient blood of Polska in their veins, blood like Ruthie's except that they believed the Messiah had already come to tell the world: "Mercy conquers justice..."

Beyond Saint Casimir's, Ruthie made out the long and wobbly pier of Orlo's Salvage House as it jutted from the end of Clinton Street and into the harbor, the place she went when Miss Bonnie's was closed to buy faded clothes and hang her feet over the side of the crumbling seawall; where her great-grandfather used to come to rest and talk with Orlo about the way it was for peddlers in the New World, hucksters who longed to open a tailor shop, maybe a storefront, but could not break free of pushcarts and ponies.

The balloon drifted higher and Ruthie's eyes followed a brick walkway to the crumbling pillars and peaked roof of a nineteenth-century shul called the Lloyd Street Synagogue.

Lloyd Street, where the Singer family worshipped on the pivot of the last dead century, back when Jews worked and prayed in Baltimore City, where Ruthie's great-grandfather came to daven long after all of his friends had left the city by death or choice.

Lloyd Street, where a five-year-old named Ruthie had gathered her last memories that made sense; where everything the child knew about the faith of her birth lay in Old Pop's face as his mourners trickled in from the suburbs to sit shiva above a store where they slaughtered chickens by the book.

It was the old man's sweat—"Pots and pans, Orlo, once in awhile I sharpen a knife or a pair of scissors, fix an umbrella..."—that put a son through night school who put a son through med school who put Ruthie in with the bluebloods of Roland Park.

And it was his legs, like the spokes of a banister, that pushed a cart through the alleys to nurture a legacy of prosperity and disintegration; a broom that swept a girl of five behind the doors in her head only to wake her up ten years later in the vestibule of womanhood, a peach gone sour.

How many patched-up umbrellas equal the bottom dropped out of a childhood?

Lloyd Street passed from view and Ruthie breathed deep, fresh air, resolving to ask her father for a hot-air balloon just as soon as she got home.

In the sky, she discovered, was the perfect place to be.

The pilot was not so sure.

All the other balloons were sailing northwest, beyond the city limits to the Jewish suburbs of cul-de-sacs, sofas covered with crushed velvet, Reform temples made of glass and steel, and split-level dollhouses where no one was ever home.

All of the balloons except one: the great inflated head of the King of Rock-and-Roll trapped in a double-crosswind pushing it east by southeast at three times the speed of the others.

"Goddamn," said the pilot.

Ruthie stood away from him, on the other side of the fuel canister, rocked in the silence of an invisible lullaby and contemplating treasure that only waited for her to claim it; thinking that maybe it suited her to become the most famous balloonist in the world, Ruthie Earhart taming fickle winds in a balloon sculpted in the image of herself.

"Goddamn," said the pilot.

In forty years of piercing the sky—as a boy with kites, a gunship driver in Nam, and a hang-glider wafting through the crevice of a valley named death—Gus had seen it all.

But he had never seen this.

Knocking back a belt from his silver flask, a trophy from a rogue who taught him to handle balloons long before Ruthie was born and Elvis had died, Gus recited an old lament behind his teeth: "I know the wind like my own right mind, and I know it can't be knowed...I want to ride a sweet summer breeze, but I don't know where she blows..."

A whistle in the dark.

There was no wind.

The skies were dead, yet Elvis kept sailing toward the ocean.

Leaning over the fuel tank, Gus dropped his face in front of Ruthie and pointed to a far spot in the sky where the other balloons had fled in a pack.

"Thar she blows, Missie," he said. "The answer is blowin' in the goddamn wind."

Ruthie blew through her teeth, more confident than ever.

The ride was pure joy.

She loved the idea that this balloon, her balloon through the wisdom of knowing how to pick your friends, was traveling to a place where the others could not, on a path denied the rest.

Below her lay the great star of bricks called McHenry and beyond the fort's tentacles, out in the middle of the channel, red tugboats with white dots on their stacks pulled freighters to safe berths as Elvis passed overhead, fast to sky tugs no one could see, the veiled hand of fate pushing Ruthie down the Patapsco.

Lost herself in the adventure, a soap bubble floating in the breeze.

Even Gus had to admit it: on a morning with no wind, blind tunnels and the baby-sitter's burden of Prissy Highpockets and her steamer trunk of condescension, with all of this, he had to acknowledge that the ride was one of the most pleasant he'd ever taken.

Except to enjoy it he had to ignore everything he knew about the way things worked. His tricks had no more effect on the balloon than the suffering of others had on Ruthie.

Every time he shot fire into the envelope to find a responsive current or did nothing in hopes of coming down to a cooperative slipstream, the balloon failed to respond, continuing out of port and down the basin of the Chesapeake Bay.

Away from everyone she had to impress, intimidate or avoid, Ruthie was at ease and free, wearing a face for no one as her true face lay open to the sky; a perception deep in the intricacies of her self-absorption that she wouldn't trade this ride for anything.

Rising in time with the sun, the balloon brought Ruthie closer and closer to the source of the world's illumination, her body bathed in a light that changed every color from far to near.

Ruthie's nut brown hair sparkled amber and gold by turns and her skin passed from pale to the luster of whipped butter.

She wore a large man's shirt, cotton colored wheat and brown and cinnamon; a garment musical with tinkling buttons of smooth, soda bottle glass, disks of mahogany and ornaments carved from tagua nuts, each trinket worth one hundred times more than the few nickels she'd paid for the shirt at Orlo's Salvage House.

A skirt burning copper and cherry lapped her knees, made fast at her waist with a gray sash elevated to silver in the sun, and a string of beads made of stained and polished glass circled her neck, sparks of sun pushing pinlight through the orbs and speckling Ruthie's throat with color.

And when the sun passed through the soft and downy flesh of her perfect ears, it turned them a luminous crimson, revealing tiny, connected veins of blue and violet life, the floodlights of history glaring through Ruthie's body and finding it uncorrupt, blameless in a way she would never allow herself to believe.

All was right in Ruthie's world because Ruthie was no longer in it.

Across from her, Gus was near the end of his wits.

"Maybe this," he said, releasing a long jet of flame loose into the mouth of the balloon, the gas burning for a full minute, bringing Ruthie closer to the fixed script of her life, the course unchanged.

Ruthie looked straight up, her mouth in a tight, open circle, her eyebrows spanning wide arcs as she blinked once, twice, three times.

Impossible!

Warbling in the shaft of burning gas stood a giant black man, a bald-headed and billowing specter beaming down at her with a gold trumpet in his hand.

"Hello, dolly!" he rasped.

"Me?" cried Ruthie.

"What?" asked Gus.

The angel's big eyes devoured the gondola.

"Any other virgins up here?"

Ruthie felt a sharp cramp just below her stomach and balled her fists until it passed. If Carla had shown up, it wouldn't have changed the answer.

Ruthie's peace had flown and her head began pounding again.

She was talking to a giant black ghost glowing inside a column of fire.

And he was talking back to her.

Gus turned off the flame and the angel vanished. Ruthie grabbed his elbow and said: "Did you see that? Did you see that?"

"Missie," he said, pulling away from her to release another jet of flame. "The only thing I see is trouble."

When the fire shot up, the angel appeared again.

"SHUT IT OFF!!" screamed Ruthie.

Gus fumbled for the lever, but the angel remained.

In the heat of his violet gaze, Ruthie sank to the bottom of the basket, looking up, when she dared, with watery eyes fixed with fear and wonder upon a massive shaft of purple, gold, and black towering above her; certain she was seeing what she was not sure was real.

Threads of gold whirled through the purple weave of his suit, a majestic messenger mopping sweat from the curve of his wide ebony pate with a white handkerchief, smiling at the child beneath him, teeth bright as a full moon on a field of snow.

"Don't be afraid," he said.

"Me?"

"Yes, child. You," he said. "They ain't made a mistake yet."

"They?"

"Them."

Rising higher, the angel filled the inside of the balloon like a purple sunrise.

"WHY ME?" shouted Ruthie.

"Shit," said Gus, his face crumpled like an old brown bag.

In almost thirty years he had lifted all manner of nuts and dreamers in the air, taking them up to be married, copulate, pass secrets, take drugs, and decide that their lives together would become forever separate the moment they returned to Earth.

But never had he played host to a spoiled brat who held one-sided arguments with the empty sky.

"Why me?" he mumbled.

But no one was listening to him.

"I don't get the whys honey," said the angel. "I just deliver the good news."

"Good news?" screamed Ruthie. "Get out!"

And the angel vanished.

But in her moment of relief, when she clambered to her knees and steadied herself on the rail with slender knuckles hard and white, Ruthie peeked over the side to find herself face-to-face with her tormentor.

Now the size of a normal man, the angel sat cross-legged with the trumpet in his lap and palms held out in explanation.

Ruthie gulped.

"Sweetheart," he said. "I don't have a lot of time and there's something you need to know."

Ruthie's eyes begged: "What?"

Gus looked over to see proud Ruthie on her knees, whimpering and talking to boogie-men, and he abandoned all efforts to manage the balloon or the day.

"WHAT?" cried Ruthie.

And the answer came.

"NO!" she screamed.

It was too weird.

Too gross.

Too sick to be true.

It was true.

"NO!!!"

Leaning out over the railing, arching her back high atop the curve of the Earth—on the edge of falling but safer than she'd ever been in her life—Ruthie shook her tiny fist at the bloated head of Elvis Presley.

"Once wasn't enough?" she seethed. "He's gotta come back? That's what this fucked-up world needs?"

"The world doesn't know what the world needs," said the angel. "It won't be him again," he said, giving away more of the story than he should have just to be done with it. "Everybody gets another chance. Even you."

"Always me," said Ruthie.

"This isn't a game," said the angel. "They like you and that's nothin' to sneeze at."

"Everybody likes me," cried Ruthie, and the angel wondered how the girl crossed the street every day without getting hit.

"It's not my job to know," he said. "All I do is bring the news and blow the horn. Now please, Ruth, are you ready?"

The sound of her name tripped a switch in her head.

"GODDAMIT! GODDAMIT! GODDAMIT! I'M READY!" she screamed. "Give me twins: Elvis and Madonna joined at the hip. Give me four and twenty blackbirds. Give me everything you've got and the minute this thing lands I'll run to the nearest clinic and kill it."

"You can," said the angel. "But you won't."

"Oh, won't I?" raged Ruthie, wondering why she just didn't jump now and save herself the trouble.

Over and over again: "Oh, won't I?" until, struck by genius, she remembered something she'd read in a book.

"I can do anything I please," she announced. "I have free will."

"You do," said the angel. "But you don't."

Pierced by truth, Ruthie's heart was bathed in a completeness she'd never known. Hymns to the silence fell down around her and she began to cry again, quietly, no fight left.

The angel pulled his handkerchief to wipe her eyes and Ruthie knew then—her cheeks wet one moment and dry the next—that it was really happening; she knew beyond thought that if a little bit of this thing were true, it must all be true.

"Okay, sweetheart," said the angel. "One more time..."

"Oh Jesus," said Ruthie.

"Uh-huh."

"Oh God," she whispered.

"That's right."

"Okay," said Ruthie.

And the angel stood in the air and turned to the sun.

Raising the trumpet to his lips, he tilted his head back against the sky and with the force of a gale blew a high C heard throughout the Cosmos; a note of full and singular clarity that caulked all the cracks in the universe and made the art of man shimmer in its frames; the single purpose of its unwounded wail painting the skies across all the Holy Lands of the Earth in rich nocturnes of purple and gold; the purity of its current short-circuiting the rodent brains of the evil long enough for their victims to find the only way out and its vibrations fathoming the depths of the sea where it was absorbed by millions of silver fish turning to jump in the other direction.

Ruthie wet herself.

She hung over the side of the basket and emptied the bile that had collected inside of her for a decade.

"What in hell is going on?" said Gus.

"God help me," called Ruthie.

And the wind whispered "that's right..."

Unattended, the balloon began a slow drift down to a peninsula called Curtis Bay, where Ruthie saw clusters of small, green-shingled houses with department store swimming pools in the backyards, kids riding bikes down the alleys and lines of wash stretched between the fences.

Vomiting for the last time, she was comforted to know that this was still life on Earth, though she mourned for a planet that had always deferred to her as best it could.

Past oil tanks squatting behind the houses and churches and bars and storefronts—life shoved into the spaces left over after the old dairy land had been chopped up for industry a hundred years ago—Ruthie could see a field on top of a hill.

The wide, green plane revealed more of itself with each echo of the trumpet's fading ring and the pilot's old confidence returned; he was eager to free himself of his passenger as soon as possible, confident like the Ruthie that was, but would never be again.

Ruthie lifted her head and the angel turned to speak his goodbye.

"No luck, no coincidence," he said. "No faith without doubt."

Ruthie raised a weak hand to wave as the angel's form bled from purple to pink to wisps of white across the sky, a storm cloud drained of its fury.

The balloon found the field and Gus congratulated himself on skills that never failed as the working people of Curtis Bay ran from their homes to see a once-in-a-lifetime prize drop from the sky.

With two hundred feet to go, Ruthie stared down at them in ignorance of the morning's second miracle: the absence of the assumption that they were clamoring to see her.

She was unaware that she even had a body, a body that had caused so much pride and pain in her young life.

"Why me?" had long passed and "what now?" loomed with one hundred feet to go.

It looked as if half of Baltimore was waiting. Housewives fled their kitchens and their husbands crawled out from under cars to stand with their children and point to the sky.

Ruthie's heart leapt with the hope that maybe they could see what she had seen.

Her eyes saffron bright, she thought that maybe her fate would be shared, her burden distributed, that maybe, just maybe, she was not alone in this thing.

"LOOK!" called a kid high on glue.

"GO TO HELL," said a man who went to Mass every morning.

"Yezus-ka-honey...," whispered an old woman in black.

Seventy feet, sixty feet, fifty feet.

"IT'S HIM!" a girl screamed.

As Ruthie strained to see the last wispy outline of her angel—particles from all the faiths of the world disseminating throughout the firmament—the people on the ground snatched her last thread of old hope.

"IT'S ELVIS!!" they screamed.

"THE KING!!!"

No one had seen the angel but the one to whom he had revealed himself.

Glancing over while landing in the center of the field, Gus felt sorry for Ruthie even as she confirmed his assumptions: Sweet Little Miss was just another over-educated straw bonnet who would never amount to half of what was expected of her, a zero to the left who talked to the air, screamed at the clouds, cried at nothing, and threw up on the promise of a safe landing.

Forty feet, thirty feet.

"Brace yourself, missie," he said.

The gondola hit the Earth with a thud and ripped a wake of sod as the balloon dragged Ruthie and Gus like a torn bag blowing down a gutter.

People raced after the sputtering head of Elvis, grabbing the gondola on the balloon's last gasp.

Ruthie crawled out of the overturned basket and her well-wishers parted to let her pass.

"God, she's pretty," said a kid about Ruthie's age, the only person in the crowd to ignore the balloon in deference to the queen who had emerged from it. "They don't make 'em like that around here."

Deaf to the chatter, Ruthie rode a wave of peace she could not name, only wanting a cab to take her home and a new angel to explain to her parents what had been explained to her.

If one part of it were true, it must all be true.

Walking a lonely road down to the real world, Ruthie looked over her shoulder to see the sky change with every step she took, remembering that the angel had said: "It changes like the air around you..."

But he hadn't said what.

The din faded behind Ruthie and a voice not her own said not to worry, that the care of Ruth Hadassah Singer was no longer something she needed to think about.

The thought took root as Ruthie's eyes opened to Curtis Bay as a place where people needed more than money to make it from one day to the next.

And the same voice that told her all was well in the midst of such a terrible reckoning said that she would come to know the neighborhood with an intimacy previously reserved for her selfish heart.

With her head out in front of her body, Ruthie hit level ground and the large rainbow glass in the windows of Saint Athanasius Church: white and green championing the inextricable connectedness of heaven and Earth; blue and red declaring the inescapable composite of beings called human.

One last time she looked back to the hill where the ride had ended and her life had begun, one more look back to Gus and Elvis, the people cheering them and a stone water tower through which all the water of the Holy Land came to be cleansed for a million waiting taps.

And in that last sweep of time dispatching her visitor beyond the clouds of just another Saturday in Baltimore, Ruthie understood why she had always held back, why she was always afraid, why she was the only fifteen-year-old virgin she knew.

For this.

So this could happen.

Ruthie's waist tightened and her nipples tingled.

A little farther, down at the curb, a cab waited and as the driver got out to open her door. Ruthie knew she was pregnant, one with the child inside of her as sure as she knew her name was Ruthie.

Red
Rain

I LIE FLAT on a bare wooden floor.

Face down.

Prostrate.

My nose nuzzling dust the way it used to nuzzle Baby.

I have felt this bad before.

Worse, even.

(Oh Baby, if I had Possession over Judgement Day...)

But I have never prayed this way before.

I saw a priest in purple robes do it at Good Friday service not long ago, face down on the altar as a lone trombone quivered across the blue notes of the passion.

Were you there?

Were you there when they?

Lord, it makes me tremble.

Tremble.

Just like Baby, before she went away.

Way up inside of her head.

Where I cannot go.

Hide and go seek.

Hide.

And go.

Baby is hiding and I am about to seek, face down in my parlor on a hot night in Baltimore, asking for strength and guidance but too agitated to wait.

Baby, why did you go away?

And leave me behind?

"God help me," I cry, a simple petition that never fails, except I doubt I'll recognize an answer if one appears.

And so I imitate the One True Theater: stretched out flat, fingertips to toes, my face against the floor and the night damp with heat; the hour late when I fell and even later now, but not as late and not as sweet as the night I poured warm water across Baby's shoulders, watching it stream down her back and over her hips, dipping down again and again and again until she sang out: "My heart has flown away..."

It is much later than that.

When I cannot take it any longer I get up and walk toward the heavy black phone on the kitchen wall, twirling the metal disc with the holes in it, comforted by the dull and groaning whir it makes as the number spins to its connection.

"Baby, it's me..."

Truth without love is cruel and she answers as if the ground beneath her has turned to sand.

I yearn for the succor of the bare wooden floor as she waits for me to say whatever it is that's so important.

I just want it to work.

Not because I want it.

But because it does.

"Baby, I don't want anything from you."

I try again.

"I just want you to get better."

There is quiet until she explains that getting better and being with me cannot take place in the same room.

Byebye.

Byebye, Baby.

Goodbye.

My ear drips with sweat as I lay the receiver in its cradle.

The dog days of Spring.

We didn't even make it to Summer.

I gave her my heart in April, she swallowed it whole in May, and began spitting it up in pieces by June.

Binge, Baby.

Purge, Baby.

Isn't it funny how it hurts so bad you want to die, but it's not strong enough to kill you?

It only kills with your assistance.

I turn off the light above the stove, wipe the sweat from my neck with a dish rag and trudge up the stairs to bed, stripping as I go, clothes dropping behind me.

The house is dark and hot and lightning sparks above the sky-light in the stairwell, a mute electrical storm streaking across pink plaster.

I am naked when I reach the bedroom.

I don't want to go in, but there's nowhere else to go.

The heat is brutal and the air is dead.

Not even a fan.

I sit with my grief on the edge of the bed, twisting before I lie down with it.

Before Baby went away, up into her head where I cannot go, I was doing the number on this ripe old room where I have passed so many moons alone.

I'm telling you I was on my hands and knees with a bucket and brush like an old Polish woman scrubbing steps on Binney Street.

Getting it ready for Baby and me.

I stripped the bed.

Slipped feather pillows from their cases.

And knelt down with a good rag and a bucket of hot, soapy water; hunched over in labor just before Baby went away, sweat dripping from the tip of my nose onto the gleaming boards, auburn knots anchored in cinnamon grain.

I ran the rag over black baseboards below walls painted ballerina pink, pink nearly as pale as the room where Baby said her prayers in grade school—not face down on the floor, nobody tells you it'll ever get that bad—Baby on her knees by the side of the bed, hands clasped, eyes closed and lashes the color of acorns brushing against her cheeks.

Now I lay me...

As we laid not all that long ago, in less time than it takes for the promise of Spring to bear the small fruit of Summer; nose to nose on a little girl bed where Baby whispered "I want you" and I answered in kind but it seems we were not talking about the same thing.

Do not expect, say those well versed in praying face down on the floor.

Expect nothing and you cannot be disappointed.

I stopped cleaning the moment Baby bailed.

Stopped sleeping in here.

A bucket of dirty water in the corner of a half-cleaned room empty of what should have been: Violets and daisies and tulips in stone jugs.

Flowers on the dresser.

On the sill.

Across the floor.

A garden, on the shelf.

Baby, you missed it: Gifts waiting on fresh linen.

Books with blank pages rich as cream.

And wands of oil and chalk and wax in all the colors for you to draw the pictures in your head.

Self-Portrait No. Sorry.

The bed is bare, stripped down to a stained, gray mattress, more than sufficient now that all I want is sleep, but it is too hot for that.

The mattress scrapes like a hair brush, the heat a rubber suit and air that does not move. I flip from side-to-side for a position that doesn't exist and a button cuts me under the shoulder blades.

Yellow light from the street passes through the open window and drifts across the dust where Baby's flowers would be.

My back dripping sweat where her presents should be.

Where mine was supposed to be.

Yet if it wasn't supposed to be like this, it would be different.

No room in Baby's head for anything but Baby and the vapors that want her all to themselves.

I turn to the window, wipe my face with a sticky palm, and stare out to the shambles of the bottle cap factory down by the railroad tracks.

The old heap shimmers over the rooftops.

A train creaks by on a slow roll to the harbor where freighters wait to receive it down at the end of Clinton Street.

And I lie alone on an undressed bed.

So what if Baby is toxic?

Her skin is fair and her eyes are dark.

Even as she warned me, it was a trade I was willing to make.

So what?

So I sweat as her caveats chase wiser voices around the room.

Neil sings: "Love and only love can break it down..."

Van preaches: "No method, no teacher, no guru..."

And Paul, that ball-busting circuit rider with his discipline of a love that never fails.

But Baby knows Baby better than I know love.

And even now I would leap from this bed to trade come-what-may just to trace the arc of her eyebrows with my fingertips.

Boy, you could be more fucked-up than your precious Baby Doll.

Right where I'm supposed to be.

And not a Godhelpme thing I can do about it.

Sweat like the grease from a skillet fills the creases along my throat and I push it down to my breast bone before wiping it on the mattress.

My mind drifts to buckets of ice, arms hugging make-believe in the hope that sleep will come before the image melts.

I roll.

I bend.

I tumble.

Baby's retreat rattles the china in my head.

Wise up, Ace.

Let go.

I reach behind to the headboard and arch my back, trying to keep any part of my body from touching another.

Sweat between my shoulders, on my scalp, behind my balls; sweat driving sweat as night brings down the curtain on another day by myself.

I am losing my...

Oooh.

A breeze.

So soft I almost missed it.

I lie still in case it comes back.

It does.

A kiss from the outside.

Oh!

Flat on my back—staring up at the ceiling in the dark—I thank God for it.

Praying to a breeze.

(Not for a breeze, I wasn't smart enough to think of that, but to a breeze.)

There it is.

There it goes.

Here it comes.

A little cooler than before.

A little longer.

I coo: Thank you.

Thank you so much.

I realize: My whole life has come down to the grace of a breeze.

Come, I whisper.

And it does.

Come back to me.

And it does.

I have no more power to thread a breeze through the night than I have to coax Baby down from her head.

But here it is again.

Cooler than the last time.

A little stronger.

A little longer.

Coming more quickly.

My lips move without sound: Thank you.

Over and over, on every wave.

Thank you.

Until I am carried inside half-a-dream.

I see the Virgin Ruthie give birth to a mute little girl she will name Gloria; I fall through the cobalt as Orlo and Leini exchange vows before a Unitarian preacher with empathy enough not to ask questions; I float with the clouds as Basilio Boullosa spends the last ten years of his glorious life painting murals of Anne Frank on hundreds of abandoned rowhouses from one end of Baltimore to the other.

In this sleep, I feel the breeze.

Kisses from a place I cannot go.

In cadence with a clock I cannot set.

Rockabye my Baby...

With a sweet blue melody.

I hug my pillow the way my mother hugged me on my first day of school, my back to the window as thank yous trail off to bubbles in the corners of my mouth.

I want nothing more than this.

And still there is more.

A sprinkling in my mind that trickles on my skin.

A scarlet tingle.

Garnet, raw, and rare.

Pomegranates squeezed to spray.

This is blood.

On my head, along my neck, up and down my legs from the small of my back to the soles of my feet and back again.

A shower of blood and an absence of fear.

Not like when you are cut.

Thick and hot and smeared along the bottom of the sink.

Not like mine.

Or yours.

Or Baby's the time she tried to...

(Baby, if you want to be wild, you've got a lot to learn.)

This is cool and thin.

A splash of crimson covering all of me.

Roit.

Erythros.

Ruber.

A shower of blood.

I know it.

Not like I knew Baby.

All that wishing and hoping and wondering.

Making myself sick.

Not like I thought she was going to be the one to sit out on the steps with me when the night is damp and hot.

To listen.

And be listened to.

The one who would be satisfied to do nothing with me.

Not like that.

I have been washed by a reign of blood.

I know it.

Like right now—clean and awake and looking out the bedroom window as the sidewalk is dried by the morning sun—I know it does not hurt anymore that Baby is gone.

Eat
and
Be Strong

LOU'S LITTLE GIRL SAT AWAY from the party, under a tree in the lap of a woman Lou didn't know, nothing around them but shade.

The child sat easily, the curve of her small back a perfect fit against the woman's chest; head tilted forward, talking and pulling blades of grass while fingers stained with blueberry moved through her hair.

Nora was getting a French braid from a new friend.

Lou watched from the porch of the big, brown-shingled house, daydreaming and deaf to the conversations around him.

A pretty woman was fixing the hair of a pretty girl in the shade of a huge tree and all he could think about was how long it had been and how it still wasn't much better.

Lou didn't know a soul at the party, not even the hostess, a neighbor who'd sent Nora home with a loaf of homemade raisin bread and strict orders that she and her father eat it together.

"No-rah, No-rah," said Lou, cutting slices for a bedtime snack. "We haven't lived here two months and you know everybody. I don't even know the next-door neighbors."

"It's easy Dad. You talk to people and if they like you they talk back."

And with the next slice, a small wooden top poked through the loaf.

Lou brushed it off and passed it to his daughter.

"Look Dad," she said. "It unscrews."

Nora twisted the lid and out popped a tight roll of thin paper that spun on the table as it unfurled, calligraphy from one end to the other.

"I can't read it," she said. "It's not printed and it's not cursive."

"It says we're invited to a big party at your friend's house, the one who baked the bread and we should bring something for the table."

"Can we bring a friend?"

"Doesn't say."

"We could call up Mom. She'd make something special to bring."

"I think it's just for us."

"Nobody would mind Dad. Really. Miss Leslie said I could bring Mom over anytime I wanted."

"Noor," said Lou, covering the loaf with white paper. "It's just for us."

* * *

Nora looked over at the house and saw her father watching her.

She smiled, said something to the woman doing her hair—who also looked at Lou staring across the lawn—and put her head down for more braids.

It's easy Dad...

Lou pulled a bottle of sparkling grape juice from a tub of drinks at the end of the porch; never having seen it anywhere but the shelf at Fresh Fields.

He moved carefully along the porch railing, turning sideways so he wouldn't bump anyone; nodding hello and making small, Queen Elizabeth waves to guests sitting around the wide porch, acknowledging them, but quickly thinking: I've got to get to that tree.

It'll be harder to break away once it's time to go inside with the food.

You can walk the length of a long porch with purpose, grab a drink, and stake your ground. But when you walk into a crowded room and everyone looks up, it's awfully hard to turn around and leave, although he'd seen it done.

(It'd been done to him.)

The only open space lay across the lawn, beyond the driveway where five barbecue kettles smoked side-by-side; past the middle of the yard where men in their early twenties played Frisbee with dogs; out under the tree where Nora and her friend had claimed the shade and quiet.

Nora caught her father's eye and patted the ground next to her, but Lou didn't want to disturb a picture giving him so much pleasure.

He sipped his juice and wandered back to the days before he and Nora were on their own.

His wife had loved days like this, the comfortable pace of them and riding home in the dark from picnics down the shore in Edgemere she'd squeeze Nora between Mom and Dad in the front seat, give her a big kiss and say how happy she was, how it was what she'd always wanted from the time she was a little girl.

Missing all that, she'd told Lou after being gone for a while, didn't add up to missing him. And be sure Nora's ready when I come to pick her up on Wednesday.

On the porch, Lou heard talk of risotto versus pasta, opinions on the last grape harvest in France, and how well the salmon were running in upstate Washington.

Men discussed the profits of shipping soft crabs to Japan, women whispered about saffron, and someone said a new book was coming out devoted to recipes for pig's feet. They said it was a love story.

Over these voices, boys with bad haircuts bragged about the number of plates they'd put out the night before with time left over to make last call and Lou realized he was the white guy in a gourmet ghetto, Daddy Macaroni at the mercy of chefs, caterers, waitresses, food writers, restaurant owners, line cooks, winemakers, importers, and the folks with the money behind it all.

He realized it in time to regret the three pounds of yellow potato salad he'd picked up at the A&P on the way over; remembering the German potato salad his wife used to make from scratch with bacon and vinegar and fresh parsley, his thoughts startled by a thump on the shoulder.

"Cute kid," said a man in a cowboy hat, pointing to Nora with his beer bottle.

Lou turned toward the man, who took a gulp of beer, choked back a belch, and started rambling like he knew who he was talking to.

"Did four hundred plates of pierogies last night, people lined up past midnight to get in. Who's got pierogies in this town besides the Polacks on Good Friday? Nobody before last night. Wait'll word gets out that the Cowboy did four hundred plates in one night.

"Was Marlee's idea," he said, rubbing a scar on his chin that interrupted his beard. "Hadn't had any since her Mom passed away and had a taste for them. That's when things happen, when you get a taste for something."

"Know what you mean," said Lou. "My daughter's always asking me for things she's got to have."

"That's her over there with your little girl. Loves kids, but loves the business more. Lotta heart. Four hundred plates. Do you know how many pierogies that is? I bet you can't imagine."

"Pierogies?"

"Polish ravioli. Marlee fills half with sliced pork and onion and stuffs the rest with fresh blueberries."

"Blueberry ravioli?"

"Oh yeah. Pierogies for dinner, pierogies for dessert. Four hundred plates later and they was still coming through the door. We were lucky to taste a few ourselves. Poor girl went to bed pooped."

The pierogi man began scraping his teeth with a bottle cap and Lou turned away to look at Marlee and Nora.

"She got up at 4:30 in the AM to drive out the road to pick fresh blueberries. Left me a love note: 'Start roasting the pork and have the dough ready when I get back.' But I got busy doing business, putting the word out, making sure the cabbies down Penn Station came by for their freebies so they'd tell the know-nothins about a good thing. Marlee comes back about nine and whips it all up."

Lou imagined her rinsing blueberries in the sink and spreading them on a table to dry.

"You stuff 'em, fold 'em over, and close the edges tight with a fork."

"Sounds like a lot of work," said Lou.

"Nothing to it," said the pierogi man. "Me and the help locked the doors at two and stayed up celebrating. Wait'll the Yups find out. Bet your ass we'll do six hundred plates next weekend."

"Amazing," said Lou, edging toward the steps, the cowboy right behind.

"I'll tell you what's amazing. This morning Marlee gets up and starts cooking for this party while I'm sleeping it off. I laid back and watched her get dressed with one eye closed. I love watching a woman get dressed in the morning."

Who doesn't, thought Lou, his own morning routine passing through his mind like laundry on a pulley.

Nora usually woke him up and he helped her get dressed, never arguing over what blouse went with what skirt like her Mom always did because he didn't know; trying to drink his coffee and pack her lunch at the same time without getting angry when she couldn't find her shoes, making sure she got a bowl of cereal or a muffin before brushing her hair and her teeth and it was time for both of them to scoot out the door.

"Nora loves to have her hair done," said Lou, straining to see Marlee hold clumps of his daughter's hair between her fingers, taking what she needed to piece together the braid. "Your friend is doing a great job."

"My friend," said the pierogi man, "can do it all except have little girls."

"She's got one today."

* * *

Ever watch dinner guests waiting for the meal to be served?

Sitting around with their stomachs growling, hopeful.

How they could eat a horse.

How good it's going to be.

How they can't wait.

Keep them waiting long enough—not too long, just long enough—
and they connect.

By the time you ring that bell, they're friends.

* * *

"So that's Nora's daddy," said the hostess as Lou walked toward the
tree.

"Yeah," said the pierogi man. "Didn't have much to say."

"He looks sad. See how he walks?"

"Don't know about the way he walks but he brought a tub of mayonnaise potato salad."

"Mind your manners. I put it in the refrigerator so it wouldn't go
bad."

* * *

"Daddy!" cried Nora.

"No-rah!" said Lou, leaning back against the tree, careful not to
crowd. "Having a good time?"

"I'm having a great time. Miss Marlee is putting my hair up in a
French braid. She said I could have it anyway I wanted and that's what I
picked. Marlee, this is my Dad. She's a chef, Daddy."

"I cook," said Marlee, putting the last braid in Nora's hair and making it fast with a bobby pin. "Glad to meet you."

"My pleasure," said Lou, glancing at the pale berry stains.

"All done honey," said Marlee. "You look wonderful. Like a big girl
going to the prom."

"Man O Mighty!" said Nora, jumping up to pirouette. "How does it
look Daddy?"

"Just like Miss Marlee said. The toppermost of the poppermost.
You look great."

"I'm gonna run in and see," said Nora, darting out of the shade and
across the lawn.

"Thanks," said Lou. "You made her day."

"She made mine," said Marlee, standing up and stretching, rubbing lines the grass had made on her thighs, dusting her bottom.

"Nora's sweet," said Marlee. "She talked about you a lot. I'm sorry."

"Me too," said Lou, surprised at the chuckle that accompanied it. "Are we neighbors? Who are these people?"

"Just Leslie, you, and Nora," said Marlee, sitting back down. "Everybody else is in the business, waiting for each other to drink too much and start spilling secrets."

"I'm just worried about spilling food in my lap," said Lou. "It's a little intimidating. Four hundred plates."

"More like three hundred, not even that," said Marlee. "I brought the leftovers here. Make sure you try some. Pierogies are always better warmed up the next day."

"Really?"

"Of course."

Of course, thought Lou.

Who doesn't know that?

Nora wouldn't sit that long with hardly anybody.

Standing, Lou said: "Do you think you could keep an eye on her while I run home and take care of something. I won't be long."

"I'd be glad to."

"Great," said Lou. "Be right back."

Lou disappeared behind a line of trees that marked the property line and Marlee ran up behind to see which way he went. Turning toward the house for Nora, she saw the cowboy grab the girl as she jumped off the porch.

He whispered something in Nora's ear and she broke free from him and ran to Marlee, out of breath.

"Where's Dad?"

"Let's go," said Marlee, taking her hand.

Out of the yard, following their quarry on the street, Marlee asked Nora what the cowboy had said to her.

"He promised me a dollar if I told him everything you and Dad talked about."

Marlee pulled Nora down behind a baby blue Pontiac Ventura and asked what she'd said back to the man.

"I told him I had to go."

Peeping over the Pontiac's long hood, Marlee hoped the little girl would always be so smart.

"There he is," she said.

"That's him," said Nora. "Looks like he's going home."

"Keep your head down," said Marlee. "We can dash up the alley and get a jump on him."

"He's gotta be going home," said Nora. "I bet he's going home to take a nap and won't come back to get me until the party's over."

"Bet you're wrong," said Marlee as they hustled down the alley. "What's the quickest way?"

"End of this alley and through a mean old lady's yard to Daisy Avenue."

They ran low to the ground, like Groucho Marx in a hurry, their blood racing and Marlee's long hair flying, not pinned up like she wore it to cook; Nora's braid sitting tight on her head.

The two of them holding hands.

Shooshing giggles.

At Daisy Avenue, they hid behind a mail box and watched Lou walk to the middle of the block and turn into a neighborhood grocery that sold fresh meat and seafood.

"He never goes in there," said Nora moments before her father walked out with a brown paper bag starting to show wet spots.

"Okay," said Marlee. "Quick now, the rest of the way."

They reached home just before Lou, hiding around the corner as he walked up the front steps and unlocked the door.

"Where's the kitchen?" asked Marlee.

"Around back."

They crept around and crawled up the back steps to the porch. The kitchen window didn't have a curtain and Marlee and Nora—noses above the sash—peered through a dirty screen as Lou emptied his bag into the sink, a tumble of clunks as the contents hit the basin followed by a whoosh of rinsing water.

"What's he doing?" asked Nora.

"He's going to cook."

"No way. He hasn't cooked since Mom left."

"Hush."

Lou took a frying pan from under the sink and put it on the stove. He yanked the hose alongside the faucet and gave the stuff he'd dumped in the sink a good, long squirt.

And then he let go of the hose, watched it snake back in its hole, and stopped.

Lou stood puzzled in middle of the kitchen, swiveling his head between the skillet and the refrigerator, glancing out the window, not seeing anything.

He remembered what Nora had hit him with at breakfast.

Cereal in the morning.

Hot dogs for lunch.

Microwave dinner.

He could hear her.

"You don't even try."

"Come on," sighed Marlee. "Move your ass."

Nora put her hand to her mouth to keep from laughing.

A small shelf beside the stove held spices from the old house, a cheap bottle of corn oil, white vinegar, and a small, framed picture of a young woman—a teenager, really—with a baby in her arms.

"That's my..."

"Mom," whispered Marlee.

Lou moved close to the shelf and talked to the picture with an old, small ache as he admired the way the young woman's eyes creased the same way as her lips.

He spoke loud enough for the spies on the porch to hear without straining.

"What did you always say? 'You just have to know what goes together, and once you know that, it works in a hundred ways.' How many times did I watch you make something out of nothing?"

Lou stepped back from the picture, clapped his hands and went to work.

He grabbed the oil from the shelf, dribbled a sloppy "L" and a wiggly "M" into the skillet and rubbed the letters along the bottom of the pan with his fingers.

He turned the gas on low, grabbed a clove of garlic gone to sprouts from the fridge, peeled and sliced it and did the same to an onion, laying them both in the oil, their perfume filling the kitchen and wafting out to the porch.

"Now a potato," said Marlee.

"He can't hear you," said Nora. "And we don't have any potatoes."

Lou grabbed a spud from the broom closet and gouged its eyes out with his thumb, running it under the faucet before slicing it with firm, quick strokes, leaving the skin on before dropping it in with the garlic and onion.

He put his nose to the pan, covered it and stood back from the stove, turning on his heels, chanting: What next? What next? What next?

See what you've you got, thought Marlee.

"There's nothing in this house," said Nora.

Lou opened the fridge and began taking out stuff and setting them on the counter: a doggie-bag of Italian sausage left over from a dinner on Exeter Street with a high school friend trying to set him up with his cousin; a supermarket salad from the day before; half-an-inch of red wine in the bottom of an old bottle; a few slices of lemon from a drink he bought Nora after school; and a package of frozen peas that'd been in the back of the freezer for weeks.

"Yuck," said Nora. "Junk."

"Not fresh," said Marlee. "But not bad."

Lou sliced the sausage and set it on the side, saving the sauce in a coffee cup. He lifted the lid from the skillet and squeezed the last drops of Nora's lemon over the potatoes, shredding the fruit with his fingers and tossing it in, the scent getting stronger, moving through the screen, making Marlee's eyes water.

"The sausage next," whispered Marlee, rubbing her eyes.

Lou stirred the potatoes into the onion and garlic—bright crescents of lemon shining through the mix—and dropped in the sausage before bathing all of it with the wine.

He put the lid back, checked the flame, and looked at the clock.

I wonder if they miss me, he thought.

Breaking open the bag of frozen peas, he shook them in Nora's Mr. Magoo bowl, dissolved the frost with tap water, and sprinkled the little green spheres into the skillet.

The sauce was beginning to bubble.

"Yuck," said Nora as her father picked mushrooms out of the salad. "Peas in my cereal bowl."

At the sink, Lou scooped an armful of cherrystone clams and ran them under water one last time, the thin edge of their shells glistening brown, blue, and gray.

"My, my," said Marlee.

"Double yuck," said Nora.

"You can pick out what you don't like."

"No you can't," said Nora. "The juice from the junk you don't like gets mixed up with the stuff you do and makes it all taste bad."

"I'll show you," said Marlee.

Lou lifted the lid once more and drops of condensation ran down to make a hot little puddle on the counter. He turned the food carefully and made space for the clams.

He made a ring of six clams inside the skillet's rim, made a square of four inside of that, and set a triangle of three within the four.

"Ba-da-boom!" he said, dropping the last clam in the center.

"Ba-da-bing," whispered Marlee.

Bringing his nose to the skillet one last time, Lou breathed in his triumph and brought the flame down as low as it would go without flickering out.

"Three minutes," said Lou. "Three minutes and they'll be smiling back at me."

"Four hundred plates!" he shouted, dancing a jig across the linoleum. "Wait'll she gets a load of me!"

Marlee blushed and lifted Nora to her feet.

"Let's get back," she said. "Anybody asks, we just went for a walk."

The
Flap Doodle

I BELIEVED THAT IF I GAVE LULU what she could not have that I might have Lulu.

And there was virtually nothing in the here and the now out of the reach of Lulu.

If you have seen this girl striding along Pratt Street—head up, hair flying above the viaduct where Balls Maggio once fished rubber balls from the surging storm waters of the Falls—then you know that I was not the first to bring her presents.

(Once, I filled her room with every product of apricot I could find, a homage to her homeland, proof that deserts can be turned to Edens.)

But more than that, beyond poetry and perishables, I am convinced that I was the first to give Lulu what cannot be bought.

Mirrors carved into propellers.

The light reflected in them.

And the breeze that gives them life.

Who am I?

The heart sick cartographer of Baltimore.

A Sephardic soul caught in Catholic marrow.

Hometown boy bearing a crown of dime store jewels atop the head of the Patapsco.

Not bad, but not enough for Lulu.

In the few months we spent together I learned that for all of her looks, her family's money, and brains busting out like liqueur from hard candy—brains she didn't even know she had yet—Lulu only wanted what she wanted.

Still I tried, wanting only what I wanted.

The desire of Lulu's heart?

Grandparents.

Just one set.

The little girl dying inside the future Nobel laureate cried for a bubbie and a zadie.

She talked about it everywhere we went.

What did I tell Lulu as I stared out the window of her pie-in-the-sky apartment to the mortal ground, fathoming my way down through leagues of night to a candy-striped pole of dipsies and doodles twirling behind the American Visionary Arts Museum?

I spun tales of lands that were old when Egypt was young.

The source of numbers.

And why a bluesman wears a hat.

I turned myself inside out to give Lulu what she will never have upon this Earth.

*   *   *

Lulu worked herself to death for other reasons (she was not sent to the New World to gather folklore) and on this night, like all the others, she came home exhausted.

A bite to eat, out of her clothes, a pass by the mirror-mirror, and down she dropped; wound-up like a three-dollar clock, staring at the ceiling with Mendeleyev and Pauling debating the elements in her head.

She lay upon a narrow bed in a corner of a room the expanse and hue of the Negev and I sat on a bar stool on the other side, perched by a picture window open to the South Baltimore waterfront.

"It's over for another week," I said, picking skin from my lips. "Let it go."

Lulu turned her gaze to a spot on the wall, her back to me and the only light in the room from the city of Basilio and Bolewicki and the Sacred Heart of Ruthie twinkling outside.

The city to which Lulu had come to stuff herself with facts and leave.

(I hated her for this, knowing that a life with Lulu would be a series of descending goodbyes—warm jets blasting off and cannonballs moving down the line—hating myself for wanting it when any fool could see that right down there, fixed in cement on Covington Street, beauty spins without purpose.

Don't they teach Einstein anymore? Has knowledge surpassed imagination?)

From my side of the room, I followed the shifting outline of her naked body, hands folded on her stomach, dark hair feathered across sheets that fastened to the mattress with small white buttons.

So not to disturb the rhythm of her tossings—Lulu in the Pre-Occupied Territories—I stared into the gathering night.

Down below rose a tower of psychedelic pinwheels, the biggest toy in the world: bicycle rims and stainless steel milkshake cups, a duck with whirring wings, bears riding unicycles and a lumberjack flipping pancakes with one hand while working a crosscut saw with the other.

Baltimore's whirli-gig was the gift and genius of a mule breeder who'd done with solder and sprockets what I set out to do with lies.

On the day his marvel was unveiled, the creator told the crowd: "It'll fool you how long it runs."

Unveiled yet hidden from an over-achiever transfixed by a spot on the wall.

"The Neilds are playing on Cross Street," I said.

(The sisters Neild were our new favorites and their black dress dramas—grade school love, older men with younger women, and adolescents riding bicycles into the summer night—were especially suited to our black box theater.)

"No crowds," said Lulu.

"A movie?"

She shooed the suggestion away.

"Sex?"

(This often happened. Often it was the only thing that happened, although I never knew when, only that there'd suddenly be room on the thin mattress for me and Lulu and a vague anger she never acknowledged; Lulu making weak fists as we rolled, landing them in a pantomime against my neck and the back of my head; elbows jerking back in fits and me lost in the plenitude without permission to call it love.

Knowing I was but her fourth lover—the first two beat her, the third ignored her—I'd catch those sad fists and pry them open, holding tight to the six digits remaining, reserving them forever in a place for me and Lulu and all the space between us.)

There'd be none of this tonight.

Lulu shifted on the bed—a cot in a palace, her head hanging upside down over the side, bare legs up against the wall, dwarfed by this vast suite that had cost Daddy a bundle to keep her safe in the American city; concrete acne upon the face of Baltimore that had reminded her father of Tel Aviv as he plotted his only daughter's future the summer before her freshman year.

Turning at last to face me, Lulu called her tune and weights began to rise and fall on pulleys in my head.

"A story."

It was the only thing that seemed to hold her and in the course of our season, I pulled some fantastic rabbits out of my ass to keep Lulu in one place.

The blackened hulk of Bethlehem Steel became the Roman Coliseum; the Bromo Seltzer tower was the Palazzo Vecchio, carried to Lombard Street stone-by-stone from Florence; and a rusting drydock on Boston Street would forever be the floating Arc d'Triomphe of the Holy Land.

"Look!" I'd say as we canoed toward the scarlet neon of the Domino Sugars sign. "Polaris."

And so exhausted my stores within days of knowing her, forced to find or make up new ones each time we were together, soon to offer the storyteller himself, not for the asking, but the taking; only to be admonished for blurting out my declarations like a schoolboy.

("Good morning little Lulu, can I go home with you? Tell your *ema* and your *abba*, I'm a little Lulu, too...")

On the rare nights we slept at my house across the harbor to the east, I'd spread my arms wide in a backyard just big enough for a rose bush and a trash can and announce, in my certainty that something existed here for Lulu beyond her impending matriculation: "All this can be yours..."

Lulu tumbled down from the bed to the floor.

"Tell me a new one."

"No," I said. "An old one."

A gust of wind swept the harbor, the whirli-gig came alive and Lulu opened to the transubstantiation spinning her way.

*   *   *

"A thousand years ago, when you were a little girl, your parents sent you every summer to live in Baltimore."

"Baltimore?"

"Yes."

"Why?"

"Because, sweetheart, this is where your grandparents live."

"Which ones?"

"Your mother's parents. They didn't get out before it got bad but they got out. On the boat they heard that Baltimore was a good town for people like them, that making a life here was a little easier than New York. They opened a candy store on Paca Street and lived upstairs, just a bedroom, a bathroom, a parlor, and a kitchen.

"Every summer—long ones, Loo, summers that began in May and lasted through September. They gave up their bedroom for you but you liked the couch next to the stove better so you could listen to them talk into the night."

"What about?"

"You were there."

"A candy store?"

"A confectionery at the corner of Paca and Warner Streets, near Camden Yards. They'd close early to take you for walks. They never closed for anything but sleep, not even sundown on Friday, but they did it for you, touching you on the arm to show you a bird, letting you run ahead of them."

"Where?"

"Where, she asks. Here, silly. Right here! You helped them roll pennies after dinner, millions of pennies on the kitchen table."

Lulu turned her palms to the ceiling.

"Could I take any candy I wanted from the store?"

"Until you made yourself sick. But you loved bath time best and made them come in with you, the three of you filling the old tub with claw feet your grandfather painted red. They let you run the water until it was spilling over the sides and you'd slide in. It was the ocean to you."

"Did we sing?"

"Every song you knew. Your bubbie would take off her watch and set it on the back of the toilet to soap you up, her hand nearly as big as your back. She scrubbed you and the Popper would put down the seat on the toilet and have a smoke, tapping his cigar into a shaving mug while the smoke drifted out the cracks in the door, admiring his wife's tookas while she worked that wash cloth between your shoulders."

"Popper?"

"That's what you called him."

"The Popper," said Lulu, pulling up her feet, sitting cross-legged on the floor.

"A regular mikvah this tub. The holy of holies."

"How much did they love me?"

(How much? How *much*? Oh baby doll, you poor thing, aren't you listening?)

"After what they'd been through, they loved anything they had left. And that was you, sweetheart. You insisted on watching the water swirl down the drain before getting dressed. Your grandmother picked out your clothes while the Popper locked up the store."

"And?"

"Out you'd go."

"Where?"

"To Pratt Street where the watermelon barges tied up. And on this day, after a hard rain had cleared all the steam from the air, the Popper bumped into one of his bunkies, goofy Balls Maggio strolling with a crab net on his shoulder. Balls treated you to the catch of the day—a bright yellow kickball."

"Show me," said Lulu, pulling her knees to her chin.

"It was as big as a grapefruit and you bounced it all the way down Light Street to Key Highway."

"I want it."

"It's gone, Loo. Something caught your eye and you let it roll away."

"Crap."

"Forget it. Your grandparents had a big surprise, something they'd been promising all summer. Every morning, the moment your eyes opened—your grandmother was already squeezing oranges into a bowl— you'd ask if it was the day. You almost stopped believing them."

"That's just what they thought," said Lulu.

"Finally the day comes, a Sunday, and it's a long walk to get there, past the spice factory—they were grinding nutmeg—down Light Street to Key Highway past the shipyard and on this day for which you'd waited so long you whined that your legs hurt and it was too far and when are we going to get there? For these old people it was just a walk in the park. They knew what it was like to be penned up."

"I complained?"

"What, you think it was somebody else they closed the store for?"

"I didn't whine."

"Well if it wasn't you, then it wasn't them. A half-hour walk to the surprise of your life and you got tired of waiting. But they weren't going to spoil it."

"I'm not spoiled," whined Lulu, rubbing her shins.

"Just around this corner. There. Look! See?"

"Yes."

"You can?"

"Tell me," said Lulu, stretching out on the floor and closing her eyes, soft gold and earthy maroon lids stretched over plump green grapes; lashes brushing high cheeks and nine freckles scattered along the bridge of her nose—so many times I'd connected those cinnamon dots with my tongue that I could trace their constellation from memory and now a girl I'd only glimpsed in pictures from grade school lay sprawled before me in the dark.

Did I want to marry this child or raise her?

"Your grandmother knelt down to take your chin in her fingers, turning your head so you couldn't miss it, whispering: 'There, Aloosh, over there...'"

"My special name."

"'Aloosh,' she said, 'what do you think?' But before you could answer, your zadie began to run like he hadn't for a very long time. He'd run faster back in the Old World when he had to, but not for fun and this day he raced the devil, daring you to catch him."

"I did, didn't I? Didn't I?"

"He let you. But your grandmother, who had never seen your grandfather run in America, stopped to watch."

"Take me," said Lulu, unwrapping a piece of chocolate she'd found on the floor and pushing it to the back of her mouth, talking as it melted over her teeth. "Take me there."

"To the whirli-gig! You got there first. Your grandfather waited for his wife and for a long time—maybe five full minutes, an eternity—you stood alone looking up at this miracle thirty times as big as you, your mouth open, head back..."

"Tell me," said Lulu, pulling her thick, black cherry hair out from the sides of her head, twisting it like rope. "What did I see?"

"A giant egg beater glittering like a pirate's jewels. A God-is-in-His-heaven wing-ding, baby. A spinning beanie of joy."

"Joy," said Lulu and she began to roll across the floor like a kid tumbling down a hill, arms tight across her chest, eyes still closed as she spun from one side of the room to the other chanting: "Simcha...simcha, simcha, simcha."

"Happy and free," I said. "The three of you—happy, joyous, and free. Your grandmother plopped herself down on a bench and pointed at the whirli-gig with her cane.

"'Oy,' she said, '*fardreyter*.'"

Lulu rolled back to the bed and sat up.

"Fardreyter?"

"'Flap Doodle,' explained your grandfather, tapping his cigar against the bark of a tree. 'Something which turns this way and that, upon which you cannot expect anything to last. An invention of America.'"

"I see it," said Lulu, sliding an index finger beneath her breasts, wiping perspiration from the spot where they attached to her ribs.

"Can you?"

"All the spinners up on top."

"A state fair in the air," I said. "A real you know what."

"What?"

"A real Lulu, baby. And just when it looked like your grandmother might try and pick a fight with your zadie over the exact definition of a fardreyter..."

"Fight? They aren't my parents. Why would they fight?"

"The Popper narrowed his eyes on the factories belching smoke around the harbor—the soap works and the sugar house and asked: 'How much more purpose can the world stand?'

"'But something like this,' he said, holding his cigar up to a mustachioed man pumping a bicycle at the very top, one of those big Front Wheelers from the last time the century turned, when he and your grandmother turned cartwheels in the Gymnasium, back when they thought they were German. 'Genius you don't insult by demanding purpose.'

"And before he can say another word, your grandmother drops her cane, starts flapping her arms and begins circling the whirli-gig like a giant condor.

"'Purpose,' she scoffed, picking up steam. 'You talk of purpose to a baby?'

"Round and round, flapping those wrinkled wings, this proper and dignified Berliner, a chemist like you, Loo, a proud citizen of the

Weimar Republic left to push Bazooka bubblegum across a wooden counter to snot nosed kids—a life she never thought she'd live to live—the Madame Curie of Paca Street gets it into her head to fly away with the pigeons and the Popper laughed so hard he liked to have died.

"'Now we see the fardreyter,' he coughed, hacking up his El Productos. The whirli-gig hummed like the breeze and your bubbie began to sing: 'Truth is beauty and beauty is truth, truth is beauty and beauty is truth, truth is...'"

"Beauty," chirped Lulu.

"But not without purpose. For a few seconds, blessed with a moment of forgetting, your bubbie believed that if she flapped hard enough the same breeze pushing the whirli-gig would lift her up and take her home."

"She is home," said Lulu, lost.

"When she couldn't make it around another time—out of breath, sweat dripping down her neck and into her bosom—your grandfather jumped up to help her to the bench. She plotzed down and you and the Popper just stared at her, wondering if she might drop dead until she lay her head on your shoulder and said between short breaths:

"'Aloosh, promise me, when you grow up, tell your grandchildren you saw me fly. Just for a moment—to the top of this fardreyter to drink kiddish from those silver cups. Not far, just from here to there and back again, but tell them: 'When I was your age, I saw my bubbie fly.'"

"I saw my grandmother fly," marveled Lulu.

"The Popper stubbed out his cigar on the bench and took you by the hand to a sagging chain around the base of the whirli-gig. He'd limp for a week after racing you up the hill but he had to outdo your grandmother."

"Why do people compete?" asked Lulu, summa cum laude boiled down to milk on a kindergarten radiator.

"The Popper stood next to the chain and stared down at you until he was sure he had every bit of your attention (you had it to give back then); your bubbie on the edge of the bench, hypnotized, watching you watching him and then he asked if you were ready."

"I'm ready!" shrieked Lulu. "I'm ready."

"He let go of your hand and...Viola!"

"Wala!" cried Lulu.

"Up he jumped, three feet in the air from a standing position singing: 'Watch me float up in the wind, do a somersault and spin...' It was the most amazing thing you ever saw and you never forgot it."

"Never," said Lulu, holding herself tight and rocking back and forth, biting her knuckles until they bled. "Never."

"For a few moments, as the sun passed by just so, there were silhouettes against the side of the museum—sunshine cut-outs of a bent old man jumping straight in the air, an impatient little girl standing still, and the amazing flying woman who loves them."

"Somebody took a picture," said Lulu.

"From one side to the other and back again your zadie jumped without taking his eyes off of you."

"The Popper jumping rope!"

"Up, Loo, up and over and back again before coming down in front of you, bending his knees like a gymnast after a great vault, you and him eye level, nose to nose until your grandmother made her way over and they squeezed you between them, laughing:

" 'Who's a fardreyter?'

" 'You're a fardreyter.'

" 'Oh yes, me. I forgot. I'm a fardreyter.'

"You'd have thought, Loo, that they'd never laughed before."

"Oh," said Lulu, doubling over. "They're squeezing too hard. It hurts. Oh God, I'm going to be sick. I'm sick and it hurts."

She pulled a sheet down from the bed and crawled under it toward the bathroom, yelling: "Why didn't we go into the museum before it started to hurt?"

"Wasn't the whirli-gig enough?" I asked, staring down as it danced in a spotlight.

"Enough for what?" cried Lulu, slamming the bathroom.

"Enough for one day," I whispered, amazed at what I'd done.

Lulu threw up twice and when she finally came out, I closed the picture window and drew the blinds.

The wind kicked up and the whirli-gig started to clank, metal banging metal as it jerked one way before abruptly changing direction.

The spotlight went dark and only the strobe of passing headlights allowed me to make out any of the do-hickeys on the fabulous spinning pole.

Lulu staggered to the bed and curled up under a blanket, her hair wet where the running spigot had caught it as she emptied herself.

I crossed the room and knelt at her side as she shivered.

(Lulu let me in, I want to be your friend, I want to guard your dreams and visions...)

She made a grunting noise and as she bored deeper into the corner I could hear the whirli-gig outside, banging against itself like a galley gong on rough seas.

The apostate, I whispered: "Aloosh...it was just a story."

Lulu bolted upright, turned and kicked, catching me across the nose with her heel, drawing blood.

"No one calls me that. I don't allow my own father to call me that. CAN YOU HEAR ME? Irish kike. Stupid American with the big show. Big lies. Hollywood. Stupid, stupid country of slave keepers and baby killers. Bury your fairy tales at Wounded Knee.

"I don't want your whirlies and your twirlies," she sobbed. "And no one calls me Aloosh."

After she'd screamed herself hoarse and threw up twice more; after I brought in wet towels to wipe the vomit from her jaw and the crevices of her ears and stripped the linens speckled with my blood; after I'd helped her into clean pajamas and changed the sheets, Lulu drifted off to sleep, her shoulders jerking back in quiet fits.

I left by the stairs, twenty-one floors down to the corner of Key Highway and Covington Street where the whirli-gig stood becalmed like a windmill on the Alhambra plain as transparent clouds drove past the moon.

I crossed the deserted highway toward the flimsy chain around it, no stronger than the ones that held the seats of my childhood swing set.

I jumped over the sagging links and back again to where I'd started.

Up: How much does she love me?

Down: How much?

Up: You poor thing.

Down: Weren't you listening?

And then I followed the harbor rim home to the Near East where high-rise condos have yet to be built and every now and then a cargo ship still comes to call on the Port of Baltimore.

* * *

I saw Lulu for the last time a week later.

To celebrate a looming graduation to which I would not be invited, I took her to see Gram Parsons at a blues club in the basement of a Chinese laundry on Eastern Avenue.

Gram sang "The Streets of Baltimore" and Lulu slew the crowd in her black velvet pants.

"Well a man feels proud to give his woman what she's looking for," Parsons yodeled. "And I kind of like the streets of Baltimore."

I tried to lose myself in the song, entranced by the harmonies and the orchids embroidered on Gram's shirt, but Lulu wouldn't shut up.

My God, how these foreigners love to argue.

She couldn't stop yakking about who was to blame for all the bloodshed back in her country and what she was going to do about it when she got back.

Who's wrong.

Who's right.

And, most important to Lulu's way of thinking, who must be made to pay.

Her live-and-let-live grandparents, the real ones who'd been gassed years before Lulu was born, would have died all over again to know where this child of privilege put the blame.

Gram left the stage and I pulled Lulu out to the sidewalk by her arm and said: "Every year in Baltimore, hundreds of people are shot like dogs for half-ass reasons that don't come close to the fever for the land of your ancestors..."

No one had ever thought to send me across the ocean to study, when I grew up you were on foreign shores if you wandered more than five blocks from your front door.

It occurred to me that if I ever saw Lulu again it would be by chance, if that, and as she got in my car to be driven home I found myself telling her that I couldn't give a shit about zealots who'd been cutting each other's throats for five thousand years.

And never again would I waste my breath defending Baltimore to her or me or anybody.

Lulu didn't say a word when I sped past her building, through downtown and up to Reservoir Hill to show her where teenage boys who can't spell the word "execution" fall to the pavement on the hour.

It was three o'clock in the morning, armed thugs on the corner beckoned with alchemies even Lulu couldn't muster and the part of me that wanted to fly to Jerusalem like a giant condor relished the danger.

I got out and rushed around to her side of the car, knocking hard on the window until she rolled it down. I took her chin in my fingers and forced her to look at fresh outlines of chalk on the sidewalk.

"There is your Gaza!" I cried as mini-vans from the suburbs pulled up to buy poison. "There's your Hebron!"

"You're hurting me," said Lulu, pulling away.

I peeled off of Whitelock Street and onto the expressway for the short ride back to her apartment when, with a tenderness for which I'd never given her credit, Lulu asked: "What did you expect?"

Eyes fixed on the road ahead, I stared at the statue of Nipper listening for the sound of his Master's Voice on the roof of police headquarters.

She said: "What did you want from me?"

We pulled up to her building and as Lulu got out I answered:

"I wanted you to set yourself on fire for me like a Buddhist monk..."

* * *

My grandparents loved me beyond the place where numbers end—I remember telling Lulu that no matter how high you can count, there's always one more—they loved me in a way that my parents were not able.

Where are you, Lulu?

Is anyone yet allowed to call your secret name?

I've got a million pennies to roll.

And today I have exactly as many grandparents as you do.

In my time wandering the streets of Baltimore, I have consulted gin mill gurus and paint brush swamis, trudging through brown fields of dust and feathers to have what no one would keep me from having.

I found it where Key Highway meets Covington Street, in late afternoon silhouettes the whirli-gig casts against the bare concrete walls of the American Visionary Arts Museum.

My dreams are more pleasing to me than spice factories torn down for parking lots, they fill me more than the ambition of girls who cut their hair to be taken seriously in the real world.

And across the seasons of lies in which I mistook stomach aches for love, I have given myself what I will never have upon this Earth.

$\mathcal{G}$ r a t i t u d e

THE AUTHOR IS THANKFUL for the help and encouragement of George Minot, Joseph Jaffa; the Great Society of 22 Light Street; Bonni Goldberg, Roger Michel, Susan Schoenberger, Joyce Renwick, Anne Edelstein, Bette Householder, Anne Haddad, Gusty Taler, and Mary Rebecca Smart; Vincent Brothers Review of Ohio, Dancing Shadow Press of Baltimore and ArtScape '94; Gregg Wilhelm, Tom Nugent; J.B. Howard and Jim Burger; the Acropolis Restaurant at Eastern and Oldham; Fr. Joseph Bonodio, Rabbi Martin Siegel, Sr. Maria Jackson; the joy of Amelia, Jake, and Sofia; the love and protection of Our Lady of Hope; and the grace of the God of Abraham.

Amen.

About the Author

RAFAEL ALVAREZ WAS BORN in Baltimore's old St. Agnes Hospital on May 24, 1958. He graduated from Mount St. Joseph High School and Loyola College on Charles Street. In 1977, he joined the staff of the *Baltimore Sun*, covering the city any way you can cut it.

Ralph is now writing a screenplay about the life of the great bluesman Muddy Waters and is at work on a novel about the history of rock-and-roll.

He lives in a pink and orange rowhouse set deep in the heart of the Holy Land.